Good writing is characterised by authenticity and a creative rigour that Lakshmi Kannan naturally has. In her stories a dying man is endowed with a distant vision to get confirmed of his final exit. A nearly blind old lady has the gift of sharp hearing to be a guardian angel for a vulnerable girl, protecting her throughout against all odds. An ethereal quality pervades all the stories by Lakshmi, providing an aesthetic charm.

INDIRA PARTHASARATHY

Playwright, Novelist and Sahitya Akademy Fellow

These are stories of everyday life and everyday people, written with clarity and simplicity. The simplicity is deceptive, for each story artfully unfolds deeper layers for the reader to discover and introspect. They convey a deep understanding of the daily conflicts that shape lives.

KAVERY NAMBISAN

Novelist and Practising Surgeon

Lakshmi Kannan has a very subtle yet forceful way of expressing her intent—be it jealousy among siblings, or taking advantage of elderly parents by children living abroad or the helplessness and loneliness experienced by senior people. Her stories are laden with remarkable empathy with the elderly, the lives they live, the decisions they make and their convictions. There is always hope even in utter hopelessness. The themes of the stories in this collection have divergent human relations and situations. The stories, told in a lucid way somehow carry an undertone of pathos, which according to me is the most significant ingredient of good stories.

PARAMITA SATPATHY

Akademi Award-winning Odia Poet and Fictionist

GUILT TRIP
AND OTHER STORIES

LAKSHMI KANNAN

olive turtle

NIYOGI
BOOKS

Published by
NIYOGI BOOKS
Block D, Building No. 77,
Okhla Industrial Area, Phase-I,
New Delhi-110 020, INDIA
Tel: 91-11-26816301, 26818960
Email: niyogibooks@gmail.com
Website: www.niyogibooksindia.com

Editor: Anwesha Panda
Design: Nadeem Ahmed
Cover Design: Misha Oberoi

ISBN: 978-93-91125-74-5
Publication: 2023

Price: ₹395

Printed at Niyogi Offset Pvt. Ltd., New Delhi, India

For Sitalakshmi, Ramdevi, Gyanvati, Neelam, Vandana and Shanti who helped me ungrudgingly and gave me the precious time, space and energy to write. My gratitude to them in our shared sisterhood.

Contents

Each time a woman stands up for herself,
without knowing it possibly, without claiming it,
she stands up for all women.

—MAYA ANGELOU

Foreword

Though the short story as a literary genre emerged much later in the arena of literature, both globally and locally, its stylistic attributes such as dramatic sequences, terse episodes, concision and linear and non-linear narration, have all been, in varying combinations, an inevitable part of the traditional practice of storytelling, tracing back to its rootedness in the oral tradition.

In the 21st century, along with the resurgence of interest in narrative poems, readers' interest in short fiction is on a growing curve, perhaps even challenging the haloed position of the monumental novel—much awarded, much read and much criticized. In terms of arboreal imagery, the novel is often like a banyan tree, with roots growing from branches, while a short story is perhaps a banana tree, delicate yet sturdy, complete in itself, from roots and leaves to fruits and flowers.

In *Guilt Trip*, Lakshmi Kannan's short stories written in English remarkably stand out due to the expertise and the experience of the bilingual author and translator, who easily traverses the distinct registers of the Tamil and English linguistic syntax, resonating in every carefully crafted line. We notice with wonder how prose is excited into poetry in the nuanced, aesthetic grace of her crisp narratives.

Such competence in wordplay is uncommon and indicates that this ability of the writer of seamlessly negotiating the genres of poetry, novel, short story and the culture-specific and region-specific signifiers, provides an aura of exclusivity. Though the stories have a pan-Indian reach, they simultaneously exude the aura and aroma of the practices, customs and culture of the people of Tamil Nadu. The occasional sensitive and perceptive use of culture-specific traditions and beliefs all contribute in the creation of themes and narrative techniques that distinguish each of the 13 short stories in this charming, well-crafted volume, subtle as a wafting tune in the air, soft as rose petals and distinct in its resonating message of human care, concern and deep empathy.

Among the varied themes of this rich bouquet of short stories, the story titled, 'Open the Gate', creates a sensation of Upanishadic transcendence, for after all letting go is a disciplined action; releasing oneself from the viscous craving to cling on to life for a while longer requires detachment. The intense insistence that the gate must remain open so that the final journey out of the known into the unknown can take place seamlessly without obstacles and hurdles, without walls, locked gates and barriers, has been conveyed in stirring short lines, electric in their precision, deep in their heart-wrenching awareness that the time of the final departure of the soul of the loved one had arrived, as it made its bid to ease itself out of the encasement of the body.

A short story may be easy to read, but a short story is not easy to write. As far as I know, till date it is only the Canadian writer, Alice Munro, who has received the Nobel Prize in Literature for her brilliant short stories. In fact, Munro has been described by the Nobel Committee as the master of the short story, while literary critics have referred to her as the Canadian Chekov. If we try to compare the short stories of Alice Munro with not just women writers in the Anglophone tradition but also illustrious women writers in India such as Ashapurna Devi, Mahasweta Devi, Nabaneeta Dev Sen, I do not think I would be too far off the mark if I conjecture that all these women writers would have responded with uncanny similarity about the compelling urge in opting to write short stories; the specific reason often being gendered, such as domestic chores, rearing children, professional responsibilities and incessant multitasking.

In her interview after she won the Nobel Prize for Literature in 2013, Alice Munro had stated with remarkable clarity about her purpose in writing, 'I want my stories to move people—I don't care if they're men or women or children. I want my stories to be something about *life* that causes people not to say, "Oh, isn't that the truth," but to feel some kind of reward from the writing. And that doesn't mean that it was to have a happy ending or anything—but just that everything the story tells moves [you] in such a way that you feel you're a different person when you finish.'[1]

Lakshmi Kannan would not have disagreed with Munro's views about the targets of their mutual writing. It is interesting to note that Lakshmi Kannan's first creative fiction in English, the novel *The Glass Bead Curtain*, was published in 2016. *Guilt Trip* is her first book of short stories written in English.

Another brilliant story by Lakshmi Kannan that once again melts prose into poetic intensity is 'Floating Free'. The close proximity of a tiny hummingbird, a legendary symbol of love and happiness to the deeply impressionable visiting scholar from India, is addressed by the protagonist as if the bird is a reincarnation:

> 'I know, little bird. I know you're my Amma who has come back from the other world to talk to me for a while,' whispered Harshi, her eyes going moist.

---

1 Maria Popova, "Alice Munro's Nobel Prize Interviews: Writing Women and the Rewards of Storytelling," *The Marginalian*, 13 Dec., 2013, https://www.themarginalian.org/2013/12/13/alice-munros-nobel-prize-interview/

The story 'As Dapper as They Come' stands out as a Good Samaritan story—the surprise element is that the story deconstructs the much-derided stereotype of a well-dressed young man, driving an expensive car who would invariably be arrogant, indifferent and could never be expected to extend a helping hand to an elderly couple in distress. The story addresses one of the central paradoxes of life: how appearance and reality can be contradictory, and that complacently taking a situation or a person for granted, can often be completely misleading.

The story 'The Colour Green' proves that variability of subject and narrative style distinguishes the versatile art of storytelling of Lakshmi Kannan. The culture shock that parents and in-laws experience when they are urged to visit their offspring residing in first world countries is both unnerving and devastating. The insensitivity of the youngsters towards the senior members of their own families, who have often retired from their diverse careers of distinction, their balancing of home, work and family in their own working years is showcased in the story, blended with indignation, protest, angst and pain.

The story 'Addigai' is centred on a rare and expensive neckpiece, considered to be part of a family heirloom. The glossary informs the reader that the *addigai* is a heavy, chunky necklace that fits close around the neck like a choker, and is usually studded with diamonds and other precious stones and pearls. One may regard this powerful story as another interpretation of appearance and reality. The story embeds certain crucial human inequities such as envy, greed, lack of grace and etiquette when suspicion and greed overpower social behaviourism that is expected to be an integral part of the upbringing of educated, affluent and cultured classes. This disconcerting narrative interrogates both class and gender responses, and unmasks those who masquerade as sophisticated members of the advantaged social circles.

Among the strikingly impressive stories in this volume, 'Janaki Turns a Blind Eye', is the longest, divided into five sections. As a long short story it explores and exposes the pettiness, greed, selfishness and unreliability of the kith and kin in an extended family. The definition of the family as a sacred space of total security and shared bonding and responsibilities is completely fractured, once again bringing into prominence how acquisitiveness, misrepresentation, slyness and pretence all come to the fore for material gain. The lack of respect for a newlywed young bride by her in-laws, their equivocation, their plotting to get access to her bridal jewellery and other expensive items, leave a lingering bitter taste long after the story has been read. The selflessness of the Christian nun is posed as a contrast, once again deconstructing the parameters of reliability and foregrounding people who have been in the periphery of one's understanding of a deeply complex world.

It is this particular insightful and incisive prying open of the inner recesses of the human mind, the individual psychosis and social behaviourism that often conjoin, clash and collide, that define Lakshmi Kannan's fascinating short stories. The stories in *Guilt Trip* swing between telling and showing and delve deeply into the diverse worlds we inhabit in the human universe.

Sanjukta Dasgupta
Convenor, Language Advisory Board
Sahitya Akademi

AUTHOR'S NOTE: A STORY-SHAPED LIFE

Short stories and poetry happen to be my favourite genres. Their brevity is an artistic challenge that releases a kind of tension that I have come to enjoy. Writing short stories is almost an edge-of-the-seat experience for me.

The literary ancestors of the genre of short story are fables and folk tales. It evolved out of these as a highly developed literary form in the 19th century and came into its own in the 20th century. Interestingly, the animal protagonists in fables behave much like human beings with the same stock traits, flaws and tendencies in their behaviour even while retaining certain animal characteristics. These function as creative links between the human and animal spheres. *Aesop's Fables* are attributed to the legendary Greek fabulist Aesop who lived between 620–564 BCE, and the *Jataka Tales* ('jataka' meaning 'birth story' or 'related to birth') of South Asia, generally placed around the 5th century BCE, were mainly concerned about the previous incarnations of Gautama Buddha. What one remembers vividly is the symbiotic relationship between the teller and the listener when we as kids listened to the stories and the adults narrated them with an excitement that matched ours, creating a charmed circle around us. We grew up on folk tales and legends that were peppered with droll humour and funny anecdotes and listened to epics like *Ramayana* and *Mahabharata*. The fact that we listened to repeated narrations of these epics without ever getting weary of the stories defies all reason.

The shortness of the short story then, is a fascinatingly indefinable challenge. Obviously, the story has to make an impact within a brief span of time. Edgar Allan Poe remarked that the short story must be conceived of in terms of a 'single effect' that is achieved with economy and a rigorous sense of relevance evoked within a 'single sitting' by the reader. Stories that are written with a cognitive unity reach us whole and linger in our mind long after we've read them. Some of the most legendary films have been adapted from short stories.

In this collection, I've put together stories that are very short along with those that take a little more space to unfold the exposition of the theme. For each one of the stories, I've followed my instincts from the dictates that came from within the story while trying not to impose a structure on it. Some stories took me to an aural realm. In "A' for Apple' for instance, I just followed the moves of a small-town boy from Karnataka who loves the sonic vibrations of rhymes and songs in his vernacular, Kannada. In a very different way, the sounds of a classical number from Carnatic music sung by a terminally ill man in a room filled with an eerie silence is what I tried to depict in the very brief story 'Open the Gate'. The story emerged with a defiantly small and tight frame and I did not want to use a single word that was redundant to the atmosphere created by the story. My aim was to stop when the story asked me to write that one last word, and leave it for the readers to reflect upon it within the crucible of their consciousness.

Some of the stories may read like flash fiction, with a single image that dominates visually. The story around them is mainly to highlight this effect. 'Guilt Trip' and 'As Dapper as They Come' were written under the compulsive power of an image. Other stories seek a slightly larger canvas to unfold and that has to be accommodated in the narrative. 'Janaki Turns a Blind Eye' is one such long story that arranged itself in five sections to mark the stages through which Janaki, a frail elderly lady, who is nearly blind, sets about executing her plan through a well-thought out procedure. I had a similar creative experience while writing 'Addigai' and 'VRS' in which the central women protagonists have to make some clever moves to salvage something that is valuable to them.

In the same spirit of making way for the forces that come from within a story, I have allowed certain paradigms that recur as tropes to play themselves out on their own steam. One such trope is a woman's equation with food and cooking, two things that seemed to emerge almost inadvertently, for they reflect how a woman is perceived by others, particularly by men.

In a world where space is gendered, any creativity per se, whether it is in the performing arts or writing, shapes a space of its own, whatever be the genre—short story, novel, poem, play or film. The author's point of view manifests itself within this space. My stories that evoke the Tamil cultural milieu mark a stagnant rural-urban divide that continues to be an anachronistic feature till date. They show people who are clearly out of step with the changing times. A majority of people, especially men, do not have what one may call an 'urban sensibility' even while they live in metros. They continue to essentialise contemporary women who have transitioned into their professional roles as engineers, doctors, lawyers, academicians, politicians or in other career choices. This regressive mindset comes into play when they interact with women in a way that often borders on plain misogyny. In Tamil Nadu, the retrograde maxim that a 'woman's place is in the kitchen and the backyard' still functions with a mind-numbing attitude, irrespective of her economic, social or professional status, or how demanding her career is.

Once the stories with food as a trope were published—'Dregs', 'Kitchen Fire' and 'The Colour Green', to be specific—I got an instant and vociferous response from thinking women readers. Living in the times of internet and social media, there was a flood of messages on social media, WhatsApp groups of writers and poets and mails sent to my personal email address. Almost all of them declared that I've articulated the 'unspoken truth of their lives.'

Another sub-text to this food-related trope is a peculiar trait that is not easy to forgive. The same people who so inextricably intertwine a woman's life with the food she prepares, are somehow incredibly obtuse in the way they cannot see—or will not see—that women have to eat too, or rather, women equally love good food as much as they do! This plain truth escapes them totally! So, I liked to reverse the picture in my story 'Annapurna Bhavan', that runs counter to the ones that portray them as mere victims of a stubborn system. This story shows how women from middle or lower middle-class sections get even with the rigid social framework. They abandon themselves to a day's enjoyment of eating out to their hearts' content, without the presence of their family watching them with censoring eyes. There is every hope that these feisty, spirited women will eventually bring about a change by asserting their basic rights on their own terms.

That a woman is expected to put out enough food—and quality food—on the table is a trope I did not resist. I allowed it to surface even if it found some surprisingly new, unforeseen contexts to renew itself. The kitchen reaches a woman with a long arm in insidious ways, and through treacherous trajectories. This may not change anytime soon. As recently as when the nation was gripped by the devastating second wave of the pandemic, a Malayalam film titled *The Great Indian Kitchen* (2021) made a quiet entry. Written, directed and produced by Joe Baby, the message of the silent, seething resentment of the woman protagonist who has the thankless work of cooking endlessly for a family that takes her for granted, spread rapidly like wildfire and got the film a justly deserved award. The film has since become iconic. Amazing, that it took a male writer-producer to project this point of view so forcefully!

That women should cook and serve the family and other visiting acquaintances has now congealed in the Tamil mindset as something very 'normal'. More appalling is the uncaring, total indifference to the woman: Is she getting enough to eat after having cooked for everybody?—this is a question they don't ask themselves. She invariably gets to eat last, and gets very little to eat. She subsists on insufficient leftovers and gets no respite from the strenuous schedule of cooking for the family.

This deplorable truth was highlighted by Dr Thiripurasundari Srinivasan, a medical practitioner who wrote in Tamil with the penname of 'Lakshmi'. In her acceptance speech for the Sahitya Akademi Award, she highlighted malnutrition as the most dominant cause for the poor health of women and children. With a wealth of clinical experience from her long, flourishing practice in South Africa, Dr Srinivasan alerted people about the way malnutrition in women and children led to serious health hazards such as anaemia, protein-deficiency and other pregnancy-related consequences. She had more disturbing data to prove that in some families, men devour even the food that is kept aside for their own children with impunity! Dr Sundari appealed to everyone to fight against this evil practice that masquerades as a 'normal' situation.

The best way to redress the balance is to begin with the family, an important micro-unit of our social fabric. A well-known young actor from an affluent north Indian background disclosed in an interview for Women's Day, 8 March 2021, how this regrettable custom is followed till date even in her family. Her mother and other women get to eat only after the male family members have eaten. In addition, they are expected to eat their food quietly, without making any noise that may disturb their menfolk who may have gone to sleep after a sumptuous meal. Only in recent times, one sees women sitting with their men for meals, and that too mostly in nuclear families in which there are no senior members to impose stern rules.

What we need at this point in time is a new poetics of feminism that can face up to the 'post'-ness of post-feminism, and can match the complexity of creativity from writers who are women. One way is to nudge feminism closer to human rights. Life cannot be tamed by ideologies and I cannot think of any writer in her right mind wanting to do that. A healthy trend would be to critique a book by granting it an artistic autonomy. Critical evaluation that sticks to a narrow agenda of declaring what is feminist and what is not can miss out on a lot of sensitive nuances.

Ideally, a writer explores themes that factor in the changing social mores with a neutral, impartial outlook. When a feminist perspective surfaces with a certain inevitability, it has more to do with an awakening to the asymmetry in life. At the most basic level, both feminism and Marxism are all about human rights. Writers open themselves to life as it unfolds in all its paradoxical profusion. The only pledge is to the truth of what is seen and felt.

Writing has helped me find my space in life. It has given me an identity that is at times independent of what I am to my family. And yet, writing works itself out of a paradox. From a very private domain, it takes me to a public sphere in which I get in touch with my readers, who in return, connect to the very private realm in my writings because it touches something in their private lives. It moves in a circle.

The term 'fiction' as a library classification has interesting implications for both the writer and the reader. Actually, a story is an effective medium that can move beyond 'fiction' to reach for the truth of life lived in all its contradictions, for we all have 'stories' to tell. From the amorphous flow of experience, certain patterns emerge that can be surprisingly archetypal. They get a sharper outline and contour if they are 'fictionalised'. Fiction helps a writer come to terms with life. This is as true about contemporary fiction as it is about myths and legends. Which is one reason why a writer comes across readers who declare, 'Oh, that reads like the story of my life'. It is indeed a story-shaped life, like Brian Wicker postulated in his book *The Story-Shaped World*[1] which is a metaphysical inquiry into the 'fictions' in novels and anti-novels. There are stories, and there will be more stories.

1. Brian Wicker, *The Story-Shaped World: Fiction and Metaphysics: Some Variations on a Theme* (London: Bloomsbury, 2014).

சிறுகதைகள்

Short Stories

OPEN THE GATE

'It's just a viral fever,' said the doctor. 'He should be fine in about two or three days,' he added, glancing at his patrician patient whose eyes were firmly closed.

'Really?' said the patient, suddenly opening his eyes. The doctor smiled at him, as did the rest of the family surrounding the bed.

'But of course, Mr Subramanium! You're going to shake off this fever in no time. Who can keep a tough civil engineer like you in bed for long? You'll soon resume your morning walks and who knows, you may even return to your golf!' laughed the genial doctor.

There was a faint smile on Subramanium's face as he nodded. The doctor picked up his bag, waved his hand with a smile as he turned to go.

Subramanium's wife Matangi and their son Ganesh followed the doctor and saw him off at the portico. They waited till his car drove up the length of the long driveway, going past the huge iron gate to turn into the main road in front of their house. Their cook, Krishnan, closed the gate and went towards the eastern side of the garden towards the rear portion of the house. Matangi felt Ganesh's arm wrapping around her back, pressing her shoulder. Gently, she patted his hand and smiled, 'Your Appa will be fine. Come Gani, let's go in.'

***

Subramanium's granddaughter Ponni tiptoed quietly to his room.

'Ponni,' he called out softly, his eyes tightly shut.

'*Thatha*! How did you know it's me?' she said, surprised. 'Your eyes are closed!'

'I can tell by your footfalls, my darling little girl. I'll recognise them from a mile,' he said, his voice barely above a whisper.

'Shall I massage your head, Thatha?' she asked. He nodded. Very gently, she massaged his brow, moving her palms outward toward his ears. Then she massaged his temples, his cheeks and focused on his head. She softly rotated her forefingers and massaged his scalp. It felt so sticky. Has grandma oiled his hair? No, it wasn't oily. Thatha was perspiring. But why? This is Bangalore in November, with a cool breeze blowing around everywhere. She gently patted his head dry with a soft towel.

'Thatha?'

'Yes, *kanna*?'

'Are you feeling hot?'

'No. Aah...I love the way you're massaging. Feels so good.'

'Here's *Patti*.'

Matangi came in with two flasks on a tray. She kept it on the bedside table before bending down to ask, 'Will you have some warm milk, just a sip maybe?'

Subramaniam shook his head sideways.

'All right. Perhaps a little later, when you feel up to it,' she said, sitting on a chair beside the bed. She smiled at Ponni.

'Enjoying the massage?' she asked her husband.

'Ponni works magic with her hands,' he said, smiling with his eyes closed.

'Matangi, listen.'

'Tell me.'

'Ask Krishnan or his assistant to open the outer iron gate.'

'Do you know it's evening now? It's nearly 7!' said Matangi, taking his hand in hers. 'If some people or cattle stray inside and get behind the bushes and trees in our garden, we wouldn't even get to know'.

Matangi gently stroked his hands. Ponni made a silent sign to say that she wanted to talk to her. She signalled that they should go out of the room. Matangi got up.

'All right. Rest for some time. Tell me when you would

like to have some milk or soup,' she said, as she quietly followed Ponni out of the room.

'Patti, Thatha's scalp is so sticky! It looks like he is perspiring, even in this cool weather. Shouldn't you tell the doctor?' said Ponni, in a soft, hushed tone.

'Really? Let me go in and check. It's strange that he should perspire now. I'll certainly report to the doctor. Come, let's go in.' Both of them returned to the room. Matangi wiped her husband's head with a soft towel. His lips kept moving. Matangi bent low over him to bring her ears close to his lips.

'You're singing!' she exclaimed, very surprised.

He nodded, his lips moving. Gradually, the sounds were audible, for he seemed to have made an effort to raise his voice a bit. But his eyes were still tightly shut.

'*Endero Mahanubhavulu...*'

In the silence of the room, they could faintly hear this *Pancharatna Kriti* composed by Sri Thyagaraja. Although Matangi was aware of her husband's passion for music, she was surprised that he should sing now, when his condition was getting weaker by the minute.

'That's very nice,' she remarked aloud. 'But you mustn't strain yourself now. Sing tomorrow, when you feel a bit strong,' she urged.

The singing continued, albeit in a faltering undertone.

Suddenly, he stopped singing for a minute.

'Matangi, ask Krishnan to open the iron gate,' he whispered.

'I told you it's past 7...'

'Just get him to open the gate. It's obstructing me. I want to go...'

Matangi exchanged a scared look with Ponni. She went out of the room to tell Ganesh. He assured her that he would get Krishnan to open the gate. After a few minutes, Ganesh came to his father's room.

'Appa,' he said, keeping his mouth close to his father's ears. 'You're singing! That's so nice. See! The doctor said you're getting better.'

Subramanian resumed his singing as his family watched, not knowing if they should let him sing. After a while he stopped, looking tired. Grabbing the moment, Matangi asked, 'Will you have some soup?'

He nodded and took a few sips.

'Appa,' said Ganesh, bending down to talk. 'Krishnan has opened the gate,' he said, holding his father's hands. 'Now take rest, Appa. Get some sleep,' he added.

Then Ganesh went out of the outer door to the portico and saw Krishnan standing beside the open gate. Without saying anything aloud, he signalled to Krishnan to close the gate after which he turned to the right and went inside the house from the front door. He returned to his father's room from an inner door, noiselessly.

'Gani?'

Ganesh panicked, O God! How does Appa know I've returned?

'Yes, Appa?'

'Krishnan is disobedient! He has again closed the gate. Sack him the first thing in the morning!' he whispered.

They stared at the supine figure, aghast. The gate was a good 500 metres away from the portico of the house. Even they couldn't hear a thing from that distance. Then how could Appa, behind the closed doors of this room, and with his eyes so firmly closed…?

'Appa…'

'No, no! Do as I ask you to, Gani. Get the gate opened instantly. Also open the outer door of this room. It's suffocating. I want to go. I don't want any obstructions', said Subramanian.

Gani opened the door of his father's room that led to the portico. It was pitch dark now. He walked the entire length of the long driveway and opened the heavy iron gate. He touched his lips with his fingers, signalling Krishnan to be silent and motioned him to keep the gate open. When he returned, he saw the scared look on his mother's and daughter's face. They relaxed a bit on hearing the soft sounds of singing again, albeit in a rasping voice.

'Aah, it's nice that you've opened the gate now,' said Subramanium.

The family watched, stunned with disbelief. The room took on an eerie atmosphere. Subramanian's singing went on for some time in a faltering voice. And then it stopped. They waited for him to continue with his singing. It was a long wait. They felt a bit scared now.

Subramanium lay still on the bed as the family waited for him to resume the song. It was a long, agonising wait. Ponni looked up at her father, alarmed. She hurried near the bed, held her ear close to the lips of her grandfather. She placed her palm on his chest and stared at the motionless figure on the bed. She spoke in his ears, 'Thatha, Thatha, talk to me. This is me, Ponni. Your Ponni. Please say something,' she said. Her voice broke as her small figure was racked by her sobbing. Ganesh gathered her in his arms and led her out of the room.

ADDIGAI

'Tanishq will be different,' Priyadarshini told herself. 'It is a large chain of jewellers. They'll surely be able to replace the two rubies in my *addigai*.'

She entered the plush interiors of the huge showroom with her husband Krishnan in tow. The sales staff ushered them in, served them water and asked if they would like tea or a cold drink.

'Tea,' said Krishnan.

'Very well, Sir,' said the man and disappeared into the interior. A woman came to their counter. She smiled and brought her hands together in a *namaste*.

'I would like to replace the two rubies in my necklace,' said Priyadarshini. 'They look a bit faded.' She took out the *addigai* from a jewel box and placed it on the empty tray lined with deep-blue velvet. Silently, the woman ran her fingers lightly over the neckpiece.

'Exquisite!' she said.

'Thank you. See the last two rubies around the pendant on the left side?' said Priyadarshini, pointing with her fingers. 'Can you replace them please, with rubies of the same size, shape and colour?'

The woman tilted the *addigai* away from the lights, then toward the lights. She examined it with a large lens.

'To get rubies of this size and shape may not be difficult, but of the same deep colour? It's doubtful. They look like ripe pomegranates! We'll try.'

'It has to be the same kind to match this, as well as the bracelets for this set,' said Priyadarshini. She clicked open a circular box and showed her the bracelets.

'They're beautiful!' said the woman.

'Priya, your tea. It's getting cold,' said Krishnan, having finished his tea. Priya drained her cup at one go and looked at the girl enquiringly.

'Actually Madam, it's not just about finding the right rubies.'

'Some other problem?' asked Priyadarshini.

'This is a genuine antique. It's also handcrafted in a closed setting, I can tell. You know, if we display this on our show window, customers will just grab it for the price given. But…'

Priya thought, *You too*? She had grown weary of hearing jewellers say, 'Can't touch it,' 'Dare not tamper with it'.

'We're afraid of working on such an intricate piece of work for a purely technical reason. God forbid, it may just fall apart, like it does at times. Madam, I suggest you wear this gorgeous beauty as it is. Nobody will notice the two rubies. They're not that faded. Sorry, we can't be of much help.'

Priya sat still, absorbing her words silently. Suddenly, she heard her mother's voice alerting her. '*Priya, always remember! Don't wear this addigai within our family for weddings or other celebrations. Wear it only on occasions that has your circle of colleagues or friends*'.

She shook herself free of her thoughts and smiled at the woman. 'That's alright. I should thank you for saving my *addigai*,' she said.

'Come, Priya,' said Krishnan, getting up.

'Sir, Madam, can I interest you in some of our newly designed jewellery? Earrings maybe?'

'Thanks. Some other time perhaps. We're in a rush,' said Priya, getting up.

***

Krishnan drove in silence for a while, glancing at Priya a couple of times. 'It's all right,' he said. 'Your *addigai* still steals the show in our office parties and social circles'. Priya smiled at him. Jeweller after jeweller had refused to touch it, and for good reason too. They were afraid of dismantling it. With diamonds sparkling in the large pendant at the centre, it was set in a classic design. Fringed with a row of emeralds, then a row of small pearls and then the row of rubies on a thick strand, the necklace fitted her neck snugly, like a made to order choker. She could never forget the way she got it from her maternal grandmother, Meenakshi, who had given it like it was an act of stealth. Why? After all, it was her very own *addigai*, given to her by her parents, the great-grandparents of Priya.

'Come here', whispered Meenakshi, although there was no one in the room except Priya and her mother. The door was firmly bolted from inside.

'Here, take this *addigai*. I've always wanted to give it to you, and only to you,' she whispered. 'So, I stopped wearing it during the last four years, hoping that it may fade away from the memory of the women in our family.'

'Patti, why're you whispering?' chuckled Priya. 'There's no one here, and most of my aunts and cousins have gone out of the house on various errands.'

'That's why I chose this moment to gift you my *addigai*, dear girl,' said her grandmother.

'But Patti, it is *your addigai*. You can choose to give it—or not give it—to anyone. So why whisper?' said Priya, mimicking her grandmother's whisper as she encircled her shoulders with her left hand.

'Shh! Naughty girl!' smiled Meenakshi.

Such a captivating smile, thought Priya. She was a marvel in her seventies, her grandmother. She could easily beat some of the younger women of the household with her beauty and charm. Priya bent down to look at the heavy *addigai* nestling on red velvet within a large box. Her mother checked the door. Oh God, what's all this drama for? Priya couldn't fathom the need for the secrecy behind the *addigai*.

'Priya, first do *namaskaram* to Patti, seek her blessings and then take it,' said her mother.

Priya slid down to the floor and prostrated herself in front of her grandmother. When she stood up, Meenakshi had another thing for her, a circular box that had matching bracelets studded with rubies.

'Oh Patti, what's this?'

'Ssh! Quiet, my child. These bracelets go with the *addigai*,' said Meenakshi. Priya hugged her grandmother. 'Thank you, thanks so much, Patti!' she said, keeping her voice low. Meenakshi placed her right hand on Priya's head and said, 'May you sparkle brilliantly in your studies and follow your dreams in your chosen career. May you always soar in the sky bravely, like a bird that has a song in its heart,' she smiled as Priya's mother stood, gazing at them fondly.

'Thank you Patti, for your blessings. They'll really take me very far. And thank you very much for gifting me this beautiful set of *addigai* with bracelets. I'll always treasure them,' said

Priya, hugging Meenakshi again. The familiar fragrance of sandalwood and camphor enveloped her. She buried her face in her saree and lingered for a while. Patti smells divine. I must remember to keep sandalwood sachets and packs of camphor between my clothes too, she thought.

'Ask Krishnan at the earliest to help you keep this *addigai* set in your bank locker,' said Meenakshi.

'Yes Patti, sure.'

***

Priya took care to wear the *addigai* only to weddings and celebrations that were within their circle of office colleagues and friends. It never failed to make a statement and start a conversation around it. She felt proud each time a well-heeled woman, who herself dressed tastefully, went all gushy to remark that her *addigai* was 'out of this world.' She would silently thank her grandmother who had passed on. Soon after, her mother also left this world. Now Priya had only a few senior aunts and cousins within her family. Ah, that reminds me, she thought. Her cousin Radha had sent her repeated reminders for the wedding reception of her youngest child, a son.

Radha was so senior in age that she could almost be an aunt. She had married into a wealthy family that was as conservative as they come. The men in the household had zero tolerance for women who are seriously devoted to careers of their own, or women who pursue what they called 'higher studies'. Why go that far? They just didn't tolerate women who as much as read a book in their spare time. On her rare visits to their household, the sexist jokes directed at Radha and women in general had Priyadarshini seething with rage. She wondered how Radha, her sisters-in-law and the other women in the household took it all with a placid face.

What shocked her even more was the way the elderly women of the family perpetuated this appalling trait by reeling off old, obsolete proverbs that were demeaning to women. As a visiting relation, Priya had to restrain herself from accosting the old women to ask, 'Why do you do this to yourself and other women? Don't you have any self-worth?' Many of the jokes and proverbs implied that women were foolish, they had no foresight and they blundered about with their work. That a woman was at best a kind of a joke to be teased about. Never mind if their women were managing the big, prosperous household well enough, supervising the domestic staff, the chauffeur, the visiting relations, the dinners thrown for the company brass and so on. After doing all that, they were not expected to read anything other than a newspaper or a frivolous magazine, and that too only after the men have finished reading them. Any woman who took more than a passing interest in the news was a curiosity to be teased about, 'Getting serious, eh? Ha, ha!'

Priya had seen this deplorable trait in the families of her other senior cousins and aunts too, all of them caught in the mesh of wealthy arranged marriages. She struggled with her silent anger at the sexist remarks until one day she chided herself, 'Why am I thinking for them? They don't seem to be bothered at all. They're happy with their silks, jewels and prosperous homes. And on the few occasions we get to meet, they're full of pity for me, for having a job and for having married a middle-class man', despite the fact that she loved her work!

'Why hasn't Krishnan arranged a driver for you?' asked Hema, another affluent cousin.

'But I like to drive, Hema *Akka*. I like to be in the driver's seat,' she quipped, hoping to deflect her mounting irritation. The implication in the phrase went over her head, for she said disapprovingly, 'See, now you've two cars. You can sell one of them off and use the money to employ a driver,' she counselled, her lips curling to work out a cost-effective budget for Priya.

Why should I mind if these women are trivialised, or made a target of sexist jokes by their men…and women? Mentally, Priya pressed the delete button.

***

'Must we go for this wedding reception by your cousin Radha?' asked Krishnan.

'I'm afraid we can't avoid it, Krish. It's a family thing, you see. Let's go a bit late, just in time for dinner and then leave quietly without telling anybody except Radha.'

'Okay, we'll stay for the shortest time possible,' agreed Krishnan. 'It's not our kind of crowd anyway. All those hard-nosed business men and industrialists. How they flaunt their political connections! The one thing that's common to most of them is their women?'

'Their women? What do you mean?' asked Priya, puzzled.

'Why, surely you've noticed the way their women vie with each other to wear the heaviest jewellery, the most expensive sarees and then spend all their time commenting on each other's accessories, as if that's their entry to an exclusive swish club?'

Priya hugged him with a laugh. 'Oh Krish, I know. I promise to leave early. Now let me go and dress.'

She selected a fine Kanjeevaram saree with a heavy border worked out in *zari* and draped it around herself. Then she wore her pearl earrings and a matching strand of pearls around her neck. She adjusted the pleats of her saree neatly in front of the mirror. She felt it called for something more. Like what? The pearls looked much too casual for her saree. Radha's female guests would be wearing glittering chokers. On an impulse, she took out the *addigai* that she had worn last week to a friend's wedding anniversary and clamped it around her neck. It fitted snugly, like her grandmother Meenakshi's fragrant hug. And it matched her saree.

'*Priya, don't wear this addigai for our family celebrations*!' the voice of her mother floated back from her youthful days. Why ever not, Amma? You and Patti left without explaining why. What's the big mystery around this *addigai*? Anyway, I can easily camouflage it by pulling the heavy border of this saree around it. No kinswoman would get to see it. Who'll have the time to see me in the bustle of the wedding reception anyway? Mercifully, it would be dark outdoors. Patti, I want to wear your beautiful *addigai*.

***

She felt secure within the crowd spilling over the sprawling lawns. After congratulating the groom and his bride, she waved to her cousin Radha from a safe distance and joined a group of people who were not known to her. Anonymity is such a comfort. She introduced herself to the women. Sure enough, two of them started making rapturous comments on her *addigai*.

'Oooh, what a beauty,' cooed the woman who had diamonds sparkling on her ears, fingers, neck and her arms.

'Yes,' said another, 'May I touch it?'

'Of course, Mrs…?'

'Mehta. But please call me Puja. This is Usha Jain. Our husbands are business partners of your cousin Radha's husband,' they explained.

'A classic piece. Now we can't get such a genuine antique for love or money,' said a third woman, also dripping with jewels. 'If I may ask, is this an heirloom?'

'Oh yes. My grandmother gave it to me,' said Priya.

'Hmm…it's classy,' smiled the woman.

For a moment, Priya felt accepted by this swish crowd. Thank you, Patti. I feel so good whenever I wear your *addigai*. It's as beautiful as you were! Her eyes went moist for a moment, recalling her mother and grandmother.

'Ah, Priya. There you are,' said her cousin Radha who caught up with her. 'I've been looking all over the place for you. Our Swaminatha Periappa asked for you. I told him you'll certainly meet him. See that circle of chairs? He is sitting there,' she pointed. 'He is 92! Do go and touch his feet.'

'Sure Radha Akka, I'll meet him before I go,' said Priya, pulling the border of her saree well over her *addigai*. She wasn't fast enough.

'Priya!'

'Yes, Akka?'

'This *addigai*, how did you come upon it?' asked Radha.

'Excuse me,' said Priya to the women she was talking to.

'I've to leave soon. Krish has to see some people tonight,' she said, turning to go.

'No, wait!' said Radha, her jaw set hard. 'How did you get this *addigai* when the rest of us were all searching for it? Patti told us she had misplaced it somewhere. And now, how come you…?'

'I stole it, Radha Akka,' said Priya. She took one last look at the stunned expression on the faces of Puja Mehta, Usha Jain and the third woman before rushing to where her husband stood, with a group of men.

'Come Krish, let's go.'

'Go? What about dinner?'

'No need, there's plenty of food at home.'

DREGS

Sheila looked out of the window in her bedroom. The Canterbury Cathedral glowed with a coppery pink light in the half darkness of dawn. How fortunate I am to see this hallowed church the first thing in the morning, she thought.

She had visited the Cathedral as soon as she arrived in Canterbury. While she looked at the majestic sweep of the arches with their classic symmetry, she could also absorb a brooding grandeur that spoke of the tragic history wrapped around it. It completely subdued her as she stood silently at the eastern crypt that was believed to have the remains of Thomas Becket, the Archbishop of Canterbury, who was assassinated by the followers of King Henry II within the cathedral premises. Soon after, he was canonized as Saint Thomas of Canterbury by Pope Alexander III. It sent a shiver through her body.

Even now, as it was then, the tussle between religious institutions and political powers continues unabated. Sheila went to her living room. From the window, she could see a steady drizzle of snow on the bushes, trees and walkway.

Oh no! Today being Sunday, she had planned to walk up to the big departmental store to shop and stock up on groceries and other essentials, and then walk beyond to the small Asian shop that sold a few Indian things. Luckily, she had bought some extra things the last time she went shopping.

Let me cook something simple and get on to writing the papers I've to present at the universities of Leeds and Hull, she thought. Tomorrow onwards she would be sucked into the week-long academic programme at the department of Postcolonial Studies at the University of Kent.

After a shower and prayers, she went to the kitchen, measured a glass of rice for cooking when she got a call.

'Hello'.

'Good morning, Madam! How're you?' said a voice in Tamil.

'I'm fine, thanks. May I know who is calling?' she replied in Tamil.

'Arunagiri, Madam. Remember, we met briefly in our Residence Hall? You had come to see somebody, Miss Betty…?'

'Betty Cunningham, that's right. How are you, Mr Arunagiri?'

'Call me Giri, Madam. Do you also remember my friend Raman, Sundara Raman, who was with me?'

'Ah yes, now that you mention.'

'Madam, both of us thought of visiting you today, being a Sunday. From tomorrow, all of us will get busy.'

'I'm very sorry, Mr Giri. I too will get busy with the departmental programme from tomorrow. Also, I've to prepare for my talks.'

'Oh. Madam, you see, our tongue is dead,' he said in Tamil.

'What!'

'Yes,' he repeated in Tamil. '*Naaku setthu poivittadhu*', meaning he had lost all sense of taste. His palate was as good, or as bad as dead! 'The food in the Residence Hall is so bland and insipid that we just don't feel like eating at all. We stay hungry, not knowing what to do. I'm longing to return to Chennai in another 10 days. I'm fed up of bread and butter,' said Arunagiri, sounding homesick.

So, that's the reason he called, mused Sheila. When they met for the first time at the Residence Hall, it was clearly the pleasure of talking in their mother tongue, Tamil. Now the same tongue has 'gone dead' and is craving 'proper' food.

'Same goes for Raman, Madam. We just don't like to eat anything. Unlike you who have a flat and a kitchen, we've just been given this one room. We're here for a very short programme, you see.'

Arunagiri seems to have a dossier on her already, with details about her accommodation in the university and her programme. Sheila thought of the advantages she had as an invited Resident Writer for a long term. She was given a fully furnished two-bedroom flat, with a kitchen and a dining area. A housekeeper was assigned to clean up her flat three times in a week.

'Well Mr Giri, like I said, I've a lot of work pending. Actually, I wasn't planning to cook anything. Just want to make some rice and wash it down with *rasam*.'

'*Rasam*! And rice!' he shrieked over the phone. 'O Madam, that'll be like *amirtham* for us. We can help you with the cooking.'

'...'

'Madam, have you disconnected?'

'No.'

'Please Madam, do let us come over. We're not here for long. We'll soon be gone.'

'Yes, yes, I know. You told me. Come over then, at 12 noon sharp. I want an early lunch and then resume my work.'

'Oh, thank you, Madam, thank you so much! We'll help you,' said Giri, sounding jubilant.

'No need. I'll manage.' She hung up and returned to the kitchen.

***

What an enforced cooking, she thought, wearing an apron

over her dress. She heated water, measured rice in cups that could be enough for three, plus a little more for her meal at night and with some luck, maybe for tomorrow as well. She set the rice to cook and paused a bit when she took out lentils for *rasam*. It doesn't look nice to give them just a watery *rasam*. Let me make some *sambar* and one dish of vegetables. That'll take care of my meals for tonight and tomorrow. I needn't cook again. She took out a larger measure of lentils, soaked it in water for a while and then set it for cooking in the pressure cooker she had borrowed from a colleague. She soaked tamarind and sat down to chop vegetables. Will fry some *appalams* too, she thought, digging into some of the things she had packed from Delhi.

She chopped some carrots, mixed it with shelled peas, took a broccoli and cauliflower, broke the flowerets and recalled the day she had met these two Tamil men in the Residence Hall, after returning from Betty's suite.

'*Vanakkam*, Madam,' said Arunagiri in Tamil, with his arms pressed in greeting her with a *namaste*. 'I could guess that you're Tamil the minute I read your name in the News Bulletin Board at our Residence Hall.'

'Yes Madam, I could also guess. I'm Raman, *vanakkam*,' said the other guy. 'I thought it's so nice of the University at Kent to have invited you this year as a Resident Writer. I heard that you write in Tamil and in English. I would like to read your books.'

She conversed with them in Tamil. They had looked so overly happy about the opportunity to speak in their mother tongue on that cold, wintry campus. Within a few minutes of their meeting, their mother tongue gave the two men the freedom to openly complain about the food served in the Residence Hall, which was an improvised kind of a dormitory in which each of them had a room for himself.

'We don't even have a facility for using an electric stove, Madam,' lamented Arunagiri. Her friend Betty Cunningham had an administrative status, so she was given a comfortable suite at the far end of a floor, complete with a bedroom, a living room, a small kitchen that was fully equipped for her needs and a washroom.

The two men held forth on food like they were famished! Chopping the last bit of vegetables, Sheila reflected if she would also feel awful in their situation. There were no good eateries within the campus. One has to take a bus to reach the large shopping arcades that had some small Chinese, Thai or vaguely Asian joints. Tamil food? Impossible! Thank god, I've this kitchen where I can fix up small meals for myself, she thought, stirring the *sambar*. It was taking a longer time than the other dishes.

Cooking done, Sheila fried a few *appalams*. She put out three plates, glasses, small bowls and spoons on the small circular table that doubled up as a writing desk whenever she was in the living room. She would spread out drafts of her writings on the table to reduce the clutter in her study. She took out two packs of yoghurt from the fridge and a bottle of pickle that was her prized possession. On second thoughts, she scooped out a few spoons of the pickle in a small cup and replaced the bottle in her kitchen cabinet. She tidied up her hair and changed her dress when she heard the doorbell.

Arunagiri, Raman…who was the third one behind them? Giri gave a sheepish smile.

'Madam, this is Senthil. He is also here on a short programme. You didn't get to meet him the other day, so we brought him along.'

'Oh. Come in.' How could they bring another friend without as much as asking me? What if we run short of food? She quietened her mounting irritation.

'*Vanakkam*, Madam,' said Senthil, hands folded. 'I hope you don't mind my joining them. I heard a lot about you,' he said.

'Really? Good things, I hope?' asked Sheila, amused. She didn't know the other two men well enough, what could they have told this third man, Senthil?

'That you're a Tamil lady from Delhi. You've come here on a longer programme as a Resident Writer and that they've given you a flat. I felt so proud to hear all that,' grinned Senthil, looking as hungry as the other two.

'Madam', said Raman. 'The entire flat has such a wholesome aroma. We could smell *sambar* right from the stairs,' he smiled.

Sheila brought out some soft drinks and sat with them in the living room.

'How is your family doing Madam, in Delhi?' asked Raman.

'Everybody is fine.'

'How does Sir manage, without you?' asked Giri.

'Sir? Which Sir?'

'I mean your husband, Madam. Who cooks for him?'

'Why, we have a cook. How's your programme going?' she asked. 'What have you seen so far?'

They recounted their trips to various places.

'Haven't you seen the Canterbury Cathedral, which is right here on the campus?' asked Sheila.

'No Madam, not yet,' said Giri.

'Visit the place at least for the history behind it. Do you know that the Archbishop of Canterbury was assassinated in this very church, after a long drawn-out fight with King Henry II?,' asked Sheila, and then caught herself when she looked at their blank faces. Stop! They don't care about any history, she said to herself.

'Let me put out the lunch,' said Sheila. 'No! Please don't get up to help me. My kitchen is very small, there's no space. I'll manage.'

In the kitchen, Sheila took out a few serving bowls from the wooden cabinet to ladle out the rice and other things and glanced at the window. It was now snowing quite heavily. Even if it stopped snowing, it would be difficult to walk to the departmental store or the Asian store. She had already used up the dwindling supply of provisions for this unexpected lunch that was imposed on her. A third guest, totally unexpected! Let me reserve some food for myself before putting these dishes out on the table, she thought.

She took out three more utensils into which she scooped out some rice, *sambar* and *rasam*, covered them and kept them in the fridge. She stashed away a few fried *appalams* in a closed container.

***

'Hmm. The food smells divine,' said Giri.

'O Madam, the *sambar* is super, tastes just the way my mother makes it,' said Senthil, wolfing down the large heap of rice on his plate.

First, it was the mother tongue that drew them to her. Now it has morphed into a tongue that says the food is like the way 'his mother makes it'. Seems to be the 'mother' of all problems.

Senthil was totally focused on eating. Giri devoured all that was on his plate and walked to the table for more. There wasn't much left in the bowls. None of them asked her to join. Let me eat before the entire meal is finished, she told herself. The rice had reached the bottom level, there were some dregs of *rasam*, but no *sambar* to speak of. And not even one token *appalam* left on the tray! One of them had opened the pack of yoghurt so roughly, the cover was all torn. She poured the dregs over some rice and joined the group that was eating in silence. They didn't as much as glance at her. The only sounds were of food being gobbled up ravenously, of *sambar* being slurped from the bowls and sounds of *appalam* crunching noisily. They're educated enough to get a chance to come here to Kent on a programme, but they didn't look up even once to see if there's enough food left for me!

They cleaned their hands in the washroom and returned to their chairs. 'Please pick up your plates, cups and glasses from the table and wash them in the kitchen sink,' said Sheila. 'I don't have a maid to help.'

'Huh? Sure, sure Madam,' said Giri. All three of them washed their plates and bowls in the kitchen.

Sheila was still hungry after eating the scraps of food on her plate. She cleaned the small table with a sponge, then deliberately kept standing, sponge in hand. They took the hint and rose to leave.

'Thank you, Madam. We'll never forget this tasty meal.'

'Yes, Madam, you're a super cook!'

'If you need any more provisions or grocery from that Asian store, please tell us, Madam. We'll get them for you,' said Arunagiri.

'Mr Giri, I don't want any more provisions because I don't intend to cook a Tamil meal anymore. I like bread, pasta, rolls and so on.'

'O Madam, we fully understand,' he clucked in sympathy. 'How can you have the heart to cook just for yourself when your husband and children are not here?'

'Madam, the next time you feel like having a proper Tamil meal, call us. Only then you'll get the mood to cook,' said Raman.

She bolted the door after they left.

'There'll never be a next time, you ill-bred *sappattu ramans*!' she muttered aloud. She tidied up the kitchen and took out an apple-cinnamon cake from the fridge. Thank god I had the good sense not to offer this for dessert. Humph! There wouldn't have been a morsel left for me! She poured a glass of cold milk from the carton, slid a cube of ice in it and took the tray to her study.

Apple and cinnamon, you're such a well-matched couple she smiled, enjoying her cake. She recalled her sisters-in-law in Tamil Nadu who slaved all day in a sooty kitchen, cooking elaborately for a large extended family. They would serve two batches of people—the sons of the household with their mother, aunt and elder siblings in the first round, then their sisters and younger siblings in the second. Both the batches devoured large quantities of food and demanded more until there was nothing much left for her sisters-in-law. Nobody cared to know if the women who had cooked their food had enough to eat. They went to bed half-hungry. Then they got up the next day to repeat the same work, cooked large meals, ate leftovers and went to bed hungry. The next day and the next… it was understood as a very normal thing for women.

All until the day Sheila fictionalised this stark truth in a story that had women readers seething with rage. Does truth sting only when it is dressed as fiction? The story resurfaced rapidly in translations in English, Hindi and Marathi in different magazines. The editors of all the magazines informed Sheila that they received a huge amount of mail from women from across the country saying it was 'their story'. The editors of the English and Hindi magazines sent her some of the response they received from readers. Each one of the readers expressed indignation and a furious protest against the way women are treated.

This is what happened to you too, Rasha Sundari Debi, mused Sheila, remembering the remarkable self-taught woman from Bengal who wrote about her life in her autobiography, *Amar Jiban*. She cooked endlessly for a large family, also served impromptu visitors who ate up all that she had cooked until there was nothing much left for her. She got so tired that she didn't have the energy to cook something more for herself. Dear Rasha Sundari Devi, unlike my sisters-in-law who had no place in the house to hide some food for themselves, you lived in a huge house as the wife of a prosperous *zamindar*. Why didn't it ever occur to you to hide some of the food in a corner for you to eat? Why?

If only you and my sisters-in-law had the forethought to hide some food for yourselves, as a basic, legitimate fee for having cooked it...

Sheila ate the last piece of apple-cinnamon cake and sipped at the chilled milk. Ah! The quality of milk in England, it's beyond compare! It's so genuine and tasty, she thought, wiping the creamy white moustache over her lips with a tissue.

'A' FOR APPLE

Prakash piled the seven flat irregular stones one over another in a vertical heap, and then moved back with his ball to hit his target. His team watched with bated breath. The other team stood on a side, waiting for its turn. Prakash squinted his eye, took aim and threw the ball. Three flat stones fell on the ground.

'Ha! Ho!' the boys cried out excitedly.

Whether his team won or lost in the end, Prakash just loved to play this game of *pittu* with his gang that was a group of small boys from a primary school. At least, it made him forget his new English medium school for a moment.

Initially, he was excited to see how happy his parents were when he got admission to an English medium school in Malavalli. It was only to please them that he agreed to move out of his dear old school in which everything was in Kannada: the lessons, the jokes, the songs, the games and the stories they heard and shared. But things became tough for him as he started attending classes in the new English medium school. And it all began with the English class.

The minute his teacher said "A' for apple', pointing at a picture of a red apple with a glowing skin on the chart, Prakash would get hungry. He looked at the apple on the chart with longing, for he had never eaten an apple in his life till date. It must be a very important fruit if one has to learn English, he thought, since almost all the English primers that he saw in the book shops his father took him to begin with the alphabet 'A', showing a shining red apple.

The family had been busy preparing for the upcoming Satyanarayana Puja. Prakash's father was getting ready to go to the big fruit market to buy things. He always preferred the big market for festivals and special occasions because it had a few wholesale dealers who sold fruits and vegetables at a price that was far less expensive than in the regular shops near his house.

'Let me come with you, *Anna*,' said Prakash. 'I'll help you carry the bags.'

'Really? Okay, get ready then.' said his father, happy with the gesture of his youngest child. 'Good, I'm getting some help this time.' he said, pointedly looking at his older children.

They finished buying vegetables and then moved over to the fruit stalls.

'Anna, will you buy apples?' asked Prakash.

'Apples! Oh my God, they're so expensive, my child. We can't afford them. I'm getting the usual fruits for our Satyanarayana Puja: bananas, papaya and jackfruit. That's enough for our purpose,' said his father, hurrying him through the huge, crowded market.

'Anna, please. Can't you buy one apple, just one?' said Prakash.

His father stood for a minute and smiled at his son. 'What's the matter, Prakash? Why this sudden desire to eat an apple? Is it because you've joined an English medium school?' he laughed.

'No, no, Anna. Just wanted to taste it, that's all. I've never eaten an apple.'

'Ah…and that's not such a big loss, is it? Come now, help me carry this bag with bananas, and I'll hold on to this big bag with the papaya and the large jackfruit. When you slice away this thorny covering, you'll find the jackfruit, luscious, golden yellow and sweet as honey! Come, we must rush home now.'

***

Prakash tossed and turned around on the mattress as sleep eluded him at night. 'I must eat an apple, at least to see what makes it so expensive. Maybe if I eat apples, I'll be a better student in the English class.' He couldn't sleep. He looked up at the roof and thought he heard the soft twitter of birds settling down to sleep on the shingled tiles of the ceiling. Then he lowered his eyes and glanced at the sleeping figures of his elder sister and brother. He got up and stealthily tiptoed out of the room toward the kitchen. The doors of the room where his parents slept were closed. They must be fast asleep. *Ajji*, his grandmother, slept alone in the room adjoining the small prayer room. He noted that she was also fast asleep. Quietly, Prakash went inside the kitchen, switched on the light and reached for the sugar jar in which his mother kept some loose cash for daily needs to pay the vendors who brought vegetables, roasted groundnuts, the occasional ice-cream for her kids or for people who ask for alms. Prakash took out a few notes and coins, stuffed them inside the pocket of his shorts, closed the lid of the jar and went back to lie down beside his elder sister.

'I'll go to the fruit market straight from school and buy an apple,' he planned, and dozed off, dreaming of a ripe, red apple.

'Prakash, get up or you'll be late for school.'

He opened his eyes to see his mother standing, with a questioning smile on her face. He turned to his left. The mattress was empty. He couldn't see his sister or brother. Prakash sprang to his feet, brushed his teeth, rushed through his bath and gulped down the warm gruel made with rice or wheat that he had every morning. He gathered his books in his bag and set off for school.

The day started with the English class.

"A' for Apple, and 'B' for Ball. Now let's make a short sentence out of these two words,' the teacher was saying.

A boy in the front row put up his hand.

'Yes, Prahlad?'

'Miss, can we also say 'B' for boy?'

'Sure, why not?'

'The boy eat an apple,' said Prahlad.

'Good. But your sentence should have a clear tense. Either "The boy ate an apple" or "The boy is eating an apple,"' corrected the teacher.

'Yes, Miss. The boy ate an apple,' said Prahlad, sitting down, looking rather pleased with himself.

'And so, children, the boy ate an apple. Right?'

'Right, Miss,' they chorused.

Prakash tried very hard to suppress the hunger pangs growling inside his stomach. He glanced around furtively to see if the ones sitting on the same row could hear the growls. Damn this English class, it always made him feel hungry. The thin, watery gruel he gulped down before setting off for school had long since vanished, even before the class started. Also, he felt lonely in the English class. Some of the students, like Prahlad, were better than him in learning English. They dressed better too, and came in neatly pressed, freshly laundered clothes. There were a few like him who struggled with English and had recently transitioned from a school where the medium of instruction was Kannada. He glanced down at his crumpled shorts and smoothened them with his hand. Suddenly, he became aware of the cash he had stuffed into his pockets. It was there, very much there.

The next class was Maths. Prakash forgot his hunger in the tension generated by the Maths teacher, with his cane ever ready to come down sharply on the palm of an errant pupil. He concentrated completely on getting the sums right. He could manage, thanks to the multiplication table he learnt in Kannada. Nimbly, he counted on his fingers as he whispered and mentally translated them into English, but his trouble didn't end with that. Today the Maths teacher wanted the students to recite multiplication tables in English. Fortunately, he had practiced a bit at home, painfully pushing back each Kannada line of the table to make way for English.

Two Twos are Four

Two Threes are Six

Two Fours are Eight

The class droned on, alert and anxious to get it right. Prakash felt that the Maths class was also beginning to sound like an English class. The other day, his sister, older by just one year, had recited some numbering rhymes in English that she had learnt. The big show off!

One, Two, buckle my shoe
Three, Four, shut the door

Prakash had learnt his numbering rhymes in Kannada long before he had even joined the previous school that was in Kannada medium.

ondu eradu, baalele haradu
One, Two, spread the banana leaf
mooru, naaku, anna haaku
Three, Four, serve me rice
aidu, aaru, beilaiya saaru
Five, Six, lentil soup
elu, entu, palyakke dhantu
Seven, Eight, a dish of vegetables
ombatthu, hatthu, yele mudhuretthu
Nine, Ten, finish and wrap the banana
ondhirendhu hatthu heegitthu
One to Ten went on like this
ootadha aatta heege mugidhutthu
to complete the game of eating.

The next two classes went off like a breeze, as Prakash was very excited at the prospect of going to the big fruit market after school. He checked the cash and coins once again in his pocket. At the first strike of the gong, he sped out and walked rapidly towards the fruit market. It wasn't too close to his school, but who cared?

He walked towards the man selling apples, but something made him stop dead in his tracks. He didn't like the way the man talked to his customers, it was so rude and arrogant!

'Apples from Kashmir, apples from Kulu Valley. Luscious apples, sweeter than sugar! You can have an apple, only for five rupees,' the man was shouting above the heap of red apples in front of him.

'Oh God, that's so costly! No wonder Anna didn't want to buy apples', thought Prakash.

'Five rupees for just one apple? That's way too expensive,' argued a customer.

'Hey! Have you ever seen the face of an apple before? This is an apple, do you hear? Not a lemon. Move on from here if you don't have the money. Don't waste my time,' he barked.

Prakash hurried out of the place and went to a fruit stall that was two rows away from this apple seller. Cautiously, he picked a small apple.

'How much?' he asked the man.

'Why're you asking?' said the fruit seller.

'Because I want to buy it.'

'Just one?'

'Yes.'

'Where's the money?'

'Here you are,' said Prakash, giving him five rupees.

The man returned two rupees and said, 'All right, pick one.'

Prakash felt happy that his apple was cheaper than the one in the first shop by two rupees. He picked a medium sized apple, ran his fingers over its smooth surface, admired its glossy red skin and went out of the first exit point in the market.

Eagerly, he brought the apple to his lips. '*Always wash a fruit before you eat*!' His mother's voice wafted in from somewhere. Prakash looked around and couldn't find a tap anywhere. He rubbed the apple vigorously against the side of his shorts and bit into it eagerly. All the suppressed hunger throughout the classes of the day burst out and filled his mouth with water. He chewed on the apple and savoured its sweetness that spread over his palate.

'Hmm…I'm eating 'A' for Apple,' he thought, biting deeper into the fruit till his teeth reached the core of the apple. It only made him hungrier.

'But there's something missing in this apple,' he thought.

He took another bite to find out what was missing. It was sweet, to be sure. But sweetness was the only taste it had. He wanted something more from the apple. He took another bite of the fruit and got tired of its uniform sweetness. Anyway, I've paid for it, so let me finish eating it, he told himself. He ate the entire apple and threw away the core.

There was still some money left in his pocket. Prakash went back to the fruit market, navigating through the narrow passages to reach the stall that had guavas.

'I want guavas,' he told the shopkeeper.

'Sure. How much? One kilo or half a kilo?'

Prakash pulled out the notes from his pocket. He had nine rupees left.

'Give me guavas for nine rupees,' he told the man.

'Pick the ones you like and put them here,' he said, taking out a scale.

Prakash selected two large green guavas that were half ripe. He knew they would taste sharp, crisp, and tangy.

'Pick some more,' smiled the man.

Prakash gave him a bright smile, and happily chose some medium-sized guavas. They smelt divine. The man weighed the five guavas, wrapped them in an old newspaper, tied up the bundle tightly with a white string and gave the packet to Prakash.

'Here you are, little boy. Enjoy the fruits,' he smiled.

Prakash smiled back at him and walked out with a spring in his steps.

Standing in a corner of the street, he untied the bundle, took out one small guava, rubbed it hard on the side of his shorts and bit into it. The fruit exploded his taste buds, tingled inside his mouth till his entire body woke up to the fullness of the guava. This must be the 25th or the 39th guava I'm eating, and yet it tastes so new and fresh with just that little touch of a tangy sourness! It's juicy, yummy, and always reminds me of a fresh rainfall and the smell of dampened earth, he thought.

His hunger was now a bit subdued. Suddenly, he was filled with remorse for stealing money from his mother's sugar jar. Would she find some notes missing? Does she count the money each time she puts in new notes or coins? He felt awful that he had to steal money to buy an apple, which was not that special anyway. Let me give the remaining guavas to my mother and my Ajji. They can cut the big guavas into pieces and share with my Anna, sister and brother. Won't my mother suspect that I stole money to buy this packet of guavas? I'll tell her that it's from my friend's garden and that he gave them to me. He took out the guavas, stuffed the pockets of his shorts on both sides till they bulged, threw away the old newspaper with the string and walked towards his home.

His mother was waiting outside the porch.

'*Mari*! I got so worried. You're a little late today. What happened, my child?' she asked anxiously.

'I was playing *kho-kho*, Amma. I'm okay,' he smiled, taking out the guavas from his pockets. 'Take these guavas.'

'Oh. These guavas look so good. They smell nice too,' said his mother, putting out the *pallu* of her saree to hold all the guavas together. 'How did you get so many guavas?'

'Amma, my friend has a big garden with lots of guava trees. He gave them to me.'

'Very nice of him. Come. Wash your face, hands and feet. Change your clothes and put out your school clothes for washing,' she said, going inside the house. Prakash followed her, pleased with his antics for the day.

'Mari! Thank God you're back. Why're you so late?' smiled his grandmother. 'Go to the bathroom, wash up. I'll give you some freshly fried *sandige*'.

'Oh Ajji, I would love to have them. I'm so hungry,' he said, rushing to the washroom.

He washed, changed and went to the kitchen. His grandmother gave him a full plate of freshly fried *sandige* with *chakli* and a large piece of jaggery. Prakash crunched the *sandige* noisily between his teeth.

'Ajji, I got some delicious guava for you, Amma and Anna. Please cut them up and have it.'

'Really? From where did you get them?'

'My friend has a big garden with guava trees. He gave them to me. Please have them,' he said, returning to eat the goodies on his plate with much relish. He went to the courtyard at the rear portion of the house to wash his plate. His grandmother was sweeping the area around the potted *tulsi* plant.

'Hurry up and wash the plate under the tap. Let's rush inside the house. Mari, the tiles of the courtyard feel so hot! Come in, quicky!' she said. She squinted her eyes and looked up at the sky.

'No sign of rain yet, although it's time for rains. Oh God, will we have one more dry summer?' she muttered.

With his washed plate in hand, Prakash followed his grandmother's eyes and looked up at the hot blue sky and then burst into a song.

baaro, baaro, Maleraaya
Come, come, Lord of rains!
balaiya thotake neerilla
There's no water for the banana grove,
huyyo, huyyo Maleraaya
Pour down, and pour on, Lord of rains,
hoovina thotake neerilla
here's no water for the flowering garden,
baaro, baaro, Maleraaya
Come, come, Lord of rains!

'Arre! Mari, how beautifully you sing,' said his grandmother, her face lighting up with her broad smile. 'Sing on, dear child. It is said that an innocent child's prayer will always be answered. May your sweet song reach Maleraaya and may he shower us all abundantly with rain, so that we'll have good crops this time.' She cracked her knuckles on the sides of her temples in a characteristic gesture to ward off 'the evil eye' that may hover around her dear grandson.

'Come inside', said his grandmother.

Prakash went in and headed toward the room that he shared with his sister and brother. He took out his book for doing the day's homework. And smiled at the primer with the pictures.

'A' for apple.

"'A' for Ajji!' he cried out aloud.

'What! Prakash, what are you saying?' asked his elder brother.

'Nothing'.

Grateful thanks to Vanamala Viswanatha for vetting the rhymes in Kannada and for Keerti Ramachandra for her help with kinship terms in Kannada.

AS DAPPER AS THEY COME

'I found him unconscious, Doctor.' she said.

'When did you last talk to him, before he lost his consciousness?'

'Hmm...perhaps 45 minutes ago. He had settled on the front seat of our car and was chatting with me normally as I drove. After a while, he didn't talk much, so I kept glancing at him to see if he was alright. Then I noticed that his head had tilted to a side, as if he had dozed off. I pulled up at the first marketplace I could see to stop and park the car. It looked like he was unconscious. So, I rushed him here.'

'Good that you came straight to the hospital instead of going home. He needs to be revived on an emergency basis. We'll do that,' said the doctor. 'But we have to put him through some tests as well,' he added, motioning to the retinue of junior doctors and nurses swarming around him. They took Mohan away on a wheeled stretcher.

Jayashree was asked to wait in the observation room. One of the nurses said kindly, 'Madam, the tests may take long. You can have tea, snacks or lunch within the hospital. We have some good outlets in the food court,' she said, before following the others.

When they wheeled him out, Mohan looked like he was asleep. *Sleep*. It's such an innocent word when viewed in the light of the ominous things that awaited him. She sat on a small stool and waited, wishing she had brought a book along. She made a mental note to always keep a couple of books in the car for such situations. It seemed to take an interminably long time. She went out in search of the food court. There was Costa Coffee, its pervasive aroma escaping right through the slit of the glass doors. Aroma is a must for coffee to lend it a wholesome taste, she thought, taking her place at the counter. It definitely adds a zing to the taste. She watched people as she waited, wondering how many of them had husbands or family members who become unconscious without any warning. What robs Mohan of his consciousness when we've been monitoring his sugar level regularly for diabetes, along with tests for serum uric acid for his liver problem? Will he regain consciousness this time or…?

She took her coffee and found a table for herself in a corner.

'*It's good you brought him on time*,' the doctor had repeated. Her thoughts uncoiled with much gratitude to the young man because of whom she could drive up to the hospital on time for the emergency treatment and the tests. The doctor gave her hope that he'll surely get his consciousness back. Or else, who knows, Mohan may have gotten admitted to the ICU as a comatose patient, like so many times in the past. How traumatic those days were! The last time it happened, she had taken him to another hospital that was much smaller than this. Nobody even bothered to assure her that Mohan would regain his consciousness, much less survive the coma.

What a morning it has been today! It had dawned like any other day, and turned into something extraordinary due to this one person, this total stranger in the marketplace. He was the most unlikely person too that one could think of approaching for any kind of help there. As soon as Jayashree had parked, she checked Mohan again. She realised that he was unconscious. In panic, her first thought was to rush him to a good hospital, but to her utter consternation, she realised that the car wouldn't start. Shops had just been opened for the day. There were a few cars. She looked for the ones with drivers. Some of them had sauntered off to the *dhaba* nearby, an inexpensive eatery frequented by drivers, shopkeepers and anyone who wanted a quick bite and tea. She explained to two drivers that she couldn't start her car, it was an emergency and she had to rush her husband to the hospital. 'Could you please check my car?' she pleaded, adding that her husband had become unconscious. One man said he would come after tea. The other one said he would come in a minute but lingered on, chatting with the men around him. She repeated her requests, but they just nodded and said, 'Just a minute, Madam. We'll come.'

She looked around for another car, with a driver. A whiff of a deodorant or aftershave or cologne or whatever floated around her. It was a very pleasant, clean kind of smell, a distinctly male cologne, she could tell. Perhaps it came from that handsome young man who was walking, dressed expensively in an impeccable cream-coloured suit, with a necktie in a nice shade of blue, but she wasn't sure. He walked alongside the *dhaba* with a brown paper bag in his hand filled with freshly photocopied sheets of paper. Then he went over to the parking lot. He was looking around, probably for his driver, she thought, and hoped that at least his driver would rush back seeing his master. The young man went to his car, a huge, gleaming beauty in pearly white, searched his pocket for his car key and then got inside the car.

Jayashree looked around despondently for other drivers who could be approached for help. The cars speeding on the road without turning into the marketplace made her feel miserable. Wish I had more knowledge about how cars work, she cursed herself. Suddenly, she thought of reviving Mohan by sprinkling some water on his face. She ran back to the car, took out a bottle of water and splashed a few drops on his face. There was no response. She patted him dry with a towel.

'Mohan, Mohan!' she said, gently shaking him by the shoulder, after rolling up the window of the driver's seat. What next?—she thought, resting her head on the wheel when she heard a knock on the window pane. It was that handsome, expensively dressed young man. She rolled down the window. The cologne/deodorant/aftershave smelt so good and somehow just right. Right? Yes! Because it was discreet and not in your face. Must get one like this for Mohan, she made a mental note of it and looked at the man inquiringly.

'Madam,' he said, 'Is that your husband? Is he ok?' he asked.

'No, I'm afraid not. He is unconscious. I have to rush him to the hospital at the earliest or else things could turn very serious. But I've trouble starting my car. Please, would you let your driver take a look at my car? I'm so sorry to...'

'Will you open the bonnet please? I heard you asking the drivers in the *dhaba*.'

'Thank you so much. I'll open the bonnet. Could you call your driver please?'

'I drove up on my own,' he chuckled. 'Just dodged the family driver and slipped out,' he smiled, revealing a clean set of teeth in a smile that was like the smile of a child, open and guileless.

'Oh! Then please take care. Your suit may get smudged.'

'Do attend on your husband,' he said, shaking his head. He completely ignored her words about his suit and repeated, 'Please open the bonnet, Madam,' quickly taking his position in front of her car. Jayashree released the top of the bonnet.

She shook Mohan by the shoulders again, gently. There was no response. She placed her hand under his nose. He seemed to be breathing normally. Then she got out of the car to see what could have gone wrong. The young man was bent over the tangled wires and engine parts. When he straightened up, he gave her a smile that was at odds with the dark, greasy grime dripping from his hands.

'Oh dear!' she cried out. 'Please don't let the grease stain your clothes. Your suit is all cream and white.'

'No worries. I was going to get some water from this *dhaba* anyway. Your radiator is heated up. That happens with old cars. How old is your car, about five years?'

She gulped and nodded. Such an accurate guess, she thought, very embarrassed. Must sell it off soon and buy a new car. I've been having endless problems with this one. The man had already walked off towards the *dhaba*. He returned with a man who carried a bucket of water and a mug. He took a mug of water and poured it into the radiator.

'Madam, please get in and start the engine.'

She turned the ignition key with a prayer, glancing at her husband on the front seat. It sputtered, but started well enough.

The young man came near the window, his hands dripping with black grease. 'It'll run now. Just remember one thing, Madam. Don't turn off the engine anywhere, not even while stopping at a red light. Keep the engine idling all throughout the way till you reach the hospital. And get the car checked once again at the hospital. Good luck!' The same smile, like he was a child.

She tried to get out of the car to thank him.

'Please wash your hands. I'm so worried that your suit may get stained,' she said.

'No Madam, please don't get down. See...?' he pointed with his eyes at her unconscious husband.

'I can't find enough words to thank you. You are a godsend. Will this man help you wash up?' said Jayashree.

He laughed heartily. 'Oh Madam, it doesn't matter even if my suit gets smudged. I always feel happy to mess around with a troublesome car or SUV or whatever.'

'Mess around?'

'Yes, literally and symbolically. You see, I did an advanced course in automobile engineering when my parents sent me to England. It's now my passion. I went through a rigorous training. I love cars, vehicles. And hmm…I've come to like the smell of petrol and grease as I fix up engines,' he chuckled. Over the smell of the grease, his after aftershave/cologne/deodorant wafted delicately.

'And please don't thank me. It has been an absolute pleasure to help you. Just get your husband to the hospital as soon as you can. Remember to keep the engine idling. Do not turn it off!' he said, summoning the man with the bucket to take it back to the *dhaba*.

He waved his right hand, black and grimy, flashing a smile. His face caught the sun and glowed with a radiance that went well beyond his skin, his complexion, his expensive clothes.

She smiled back and waved her hand, reversed the car, got on to the main road and slowed a bit to look at him. There he was, still standing on the same spot, waving and showing a thumbs-up sign. The unsullied smile of a child sat well on his adult body, all clad in cream and white, bathed in the sunlight. Jayashree took one last look at that glowing figure.

She reached the hospital and signed the papers for Mohan to be admitted to the Emergency.

'Unconscious,' noted a doctor. 'His name, age, medical history…?' he was asking, writing rapidly on the pad as she reeled off the crucial information.

***

Jayashree finished her coffee and returned to the observation room. They had already brought him in. A nurse stood beside his bed and smiled at her. She nodded at her and looked at the supine figure of her husband. He looked like he was in a deep slumber. She sat on the narrow stool beside the bed and waited. The doctor came in with his entourage.

'It's encephalopathy,' declared the doctor, finally.

'What?'

'His cognitive functions are severely impaired. The brain scan we took shows dry patches. Haven't you noticed a change in the way he speaks, behaves or talks?' he asked.

She nodded silently. The diagnosis explained a whole lot about Mohan. Of late, he was getting forgetful and disoriented which was alarming, as was his inability to complete his sentences. Added to that was the way he became unconscious so frequently. She would think he is just tired and has dozed off on his chair, only to realise that he had lost consciousness. She recalled the various trips to other hospitals. Today, she had gotten a definitive diagnosis for Mohan's condition finally.

'We won't admit him right away,' the doctor was saying. 'Because we've hope that he'll regain consciousness. We'll observe him for some time. Please wait. Maybe we can discharge him. Then you can take him home,' he said, gently patting Jayashree on the shoulder. 'Don't worry too much. Like I said, it's good you brought him to us on time.'

'Otherwise?' I asked.

'Sometimes a patient can slip into a coma.'

'Doctor, it happened several times! Two years back he went into a coma for about five days, imagine!'

'Yes. I noted that in his case history.'

'At that time it was diagnosed as hepatic coma. He had two virulent attacks of jaundice, you see. The second one nearly damaged his liver.'

He shook his head sideways even as he said, 'I saw all that in his case history. But now, the findings are even more serious. It's a sure case of encephalopathy, according to the latest neurological report. So please be careful not to take him out anywhere too far from your home. You may not always be lucky to bring him to the hospital on time, like now,' he advised.

'Yes, Doctor. I'll remember that. Thanks a lot.'

That face, like a child, above the immaculate cream-coloured suit, the brown polished shoes, the deodorant/aftershave/cologne wafting above the greasy, grimy entrails of the car…Emerging from all those incongruous images was a young man who had this ardent wish to help. He looked so complete in his joy, fixing up an errant old car to help a woman in distress. He stood there till she started the car, got on to the main road, and waved his hand with a thumbs up sign, a luminous presence in the sunshine.

KITCHEN FIRE

Padma rushed through her lunch in the Mess and went out. She started walking briskly when Jaswinder caught up with her.

'Rushing back to the Institute? I'm also in a hurry. Have to prepare for my Status Report for the Thursday seminar this week. You must attend, Padma.'

'Definitely, Jassie. Right now, I'm going to my flat. My husband is quite unwell. I'll give him soup with something light and then come over. Have a pile of work to catch up on.'

'Oh, I'm so sorry! Raghu-ji does look weak. It seems to be a big strain for him to even walk up to the Mess for lunch.'

'It is, actually. But I let him come occasionally, just for a change of scene. That way he can meet my friends too. For dinner, we have something simple at home. It's such a dilemma. I couldn't leave him back in Delhi because he has serious health issues. We have no one in the family to look after him in my absence. And it's very difficult if I take him out with me. Risky too, when I think of us being up here, on the hills!'

Suddenly, Jaswinder stopped walking and hugged Padma. 'Still, you're batting fine, dear girl. Getting a Fellowship at the IIAS, Shimla is in itself so competitive. Just complete your basic research, take the stuff home to Delhi and write your book. Don't worry. Raghu-ji will get better soon with you looking after him so caringly.'

'You're such a pet, Jassie. Okay, now I have to go down the slopes on the left for my flat. See you soon.'

***

Raghuraman was in bed with a mild fever.

'Hi Raghu,' said Padma on her way to the kitchen. She opened a sachet of sweet corn soup, made two *roti*s on the small stove and arranged them on a tray with a bowl of vegetables that she had prepared in the morning. She kept a small cup of rice with a pack of yoghurt and took them to the bedroom. Raghu ate the soup. 'Take this after your lunch,' she said, giving him a paracetamol.

'You must eat properly Raghu, or you'll become weak,' she said. He smiled as he took a spoonful of vegetable with his *roti*.

'I'll have to go now. Will you bolt the door?'

Padma climbed up the ascent, then walked on a long narrow tree-lined path and reached the Institute. At the lobby, she requested the receptionist to call her if she got a message from her husband. 'He is unwell, he has fever,' she added.

Padma went towards the library when someone said in Tamil, 'Hello Madam, *vanakkam*. I'm Murugesan from Thittakudi.'

'*Vanakkam*,' replied Padma in Tamil. 'Thittakudi is in…?'

'In Tamil Nadu, Madam. Cuddalore district.'

'Oh.'

'So nice to know that you're also Tamil. Sir told us.'

'Which Sir?'

'Your husband Madam, Raghuraman Sir. Very nice man. We met him some days back. He said you're also Tamil. We thought you were Punjabi,' he grinned.

'Really?' she laughed and looked at her *salwar* suit, her preferred outfit for work. She found sarees cumbersome to negotiate her way through the hilly terrain of the estate around the Indian Institute of Advanced Study at Summer Hill, Shimla.

'Heh, heh…sorry, it's our mistake, Madam,' said the second man who caught up with them. '*Vanakkam*. I'm Venkata Raghavan from Namakkal.'

Another man rushed towards them, panting. '*Vanakkam* Madam, I've been wanting to meet you. I'm Veluchami. I teach in a college in Chengalpattu. I didn't see Sir today in the Mess.'

'He is not well. Has fever. You are all…?'

'We're Associate Fellows working for our MPhil. We're here for a month only.'

'Where are you from, Madam?' asked Veluchami.

'From Delhi.'

'That we know. But you're originally from?'

'I'm from Bangalore.'

'But you're Tamil, it can't be your *ooru*. Which is your home town?'

'I grew up in Bangalore. Well, nice meeting you all,' said Padma and went into the library.

***

The next few hours she got totally immersed in reading and referencing data with dates. History does not forgive mistakes in dates! And this place is such a treasure trove to authenticate facts and dates. It's such a pity Raghu's health is poor. I get very worried about what I would do in the hills should he fall ill. A drive down to Delhi takes so many hours… Padma tried to banish the worries from her mind and concentrate on her research. She got up once to call Raghu. He said he had lunch and was watching cricket on TV. Good we bought a small TV, otherwise he would be so bored, thought Padma, selecting a few books for photocopying. She took the copies back to her desk, arranged and stapled them. Around 6 pm, she stuffed everything in her shoulder bag and left for her flat.

'Hi Raghu!' she said, stepping into their home for a year. 'Do you feel better? Took a nap? Come, let's have some tea.'

'Why don't you freshen up first? Tea can wait,' he said.

'No, Raghu. I want some tea too. Then I'll fix something simple for our dinner and focus on my work. Have a pile of notes to arrange, collate and study. I'll quickly wash my face and be right back,' she said, rushing to the washroom.

Back in the kitchen, she arranged a tray with a pot of hot tea, covered it with a woollen tea cosy, put out some biscuits and salty snacks and took it to the balcony. They loved sipping hot ginger tea, looking at the distant range of hills and the lush *deodar* trees.

'How was your day, Padma? Found the references you wanted?' asked Raghuraman.

'Enough to bury myself in! I took some photocopies, will study them tonight. I must complete at least three-fourths of my project before we leave for Delhi.'

'You will, don't worry.'

Can he hold on for the next few months without falling grievously ill like he did last year? she wondered, getting up. He slipped into what was diagnosed as hepatic coma and was in ICU for four days. That was when Padma had seriously considered if she should resume her work in Shimla or give up her fellowship half way. Thank God for her nice peers and very caring seniors. They urged her not to give up, and here she was, continuing from where she left off.

Raghuraman helped her with dinner. He chopped string beans and carrots and washed the rice. Padma cooked rice on the electric heater and made their favourite *kuzhambu* over the small kerosene stove they bought as soon as they came to Shimla.

'Don't make *rotis*,' said Raghu. 'We'll have rice, and then fruits with the custard you made this morning,' said Raghu.

The two of them quietly enjoyed their simple meal. Padma's shoulders and arms ached when she cleared the table. She gathered the plates and utensils and kept them around the kitchen sink. The maid will wash them in the morning. Wiping her hand with a towel, she placed the inside of her palm on Raghuraman's forehead. It felt cool.

'I feel so much better,' he smiled. 'I'll come to the Mess tomorrow for lunch.'

'Are you sure?'

'Of course! I would like to chat with the other Fellows. I'm bored of staying at home for three days.'

Padma settled with her work. For the next two hours, she was oblivious of anything around her except the faint sounds of the TV from the next room. It's easy to just luxuriate in a wealth of research. Easier still to bite off more than one can chew, she reflected, looking out of the window at the darkening sky. Someday soon, she would have to draft a skeletal outline of her project. That'll help me keep a tight rein on the wanderings of my mind. Whatever is extra to my project can be stashed away for future. Home is the best place for me to think, plan and write the drafts.

***

'*Vanakkam*, Madam,' said someone in a hushed voice, inside the book stacks of the library.

'*Vanakkam*, Mr Veluchami. Good morning,' replied Padma softly. She took out two books and reached her usual place at a corner of the large table. She took down some points in her writing pad and marked a few pages for photocopy. When she looked up, she could see Venkata Raghavan and Murugesan hovering around Veluchami who had just emerged from the stacks. They folded their hands in her direction, their faces lit up by broad smiles. Padma nodded and smiled back, then bent over her books. No time for small talk. She was already lagging far behind her time targets. A nagging worry ate her up. The last time they had gone home to Delhi, Raghu had fallen so ill that she was flitting between home and hospital. Oh, I must exorcise my mind of these frightening memories, she thought and got immersed in her books.

'Not hungry?'

'Jassie! Just give me a minute. I'll mark these books 'Reserved' and walk with you to the Mess.'

'Okay'.

They walked past the Institute down the lane that wound its way to the Mess. Other Fellows were also walking in twos and threes.

'How is your Status Report for the Thursday seminar? All done?' asked Padma.

'Not really,' laughed Jaswinder. 'I've written a draft but it doesn't read very well. I'll put it away for a while and polish it soon.'

'You have time, don't worry. It'll come out well when you read it finally,' assured Padma.

'Look! There's Raghu-ji far ahead of us, walking slowly toward the Mess. There are some people with him, the Associate Fellows from the South,' said Jaswinder.

Padma spotted Raghuraman. Venkata Raghavan, Murugesan and Veluchami were with him along with Sunil Yadav, the Associate Fellow from Patna.

'Yes. Raghu wanted to lunch at the Mess today. He got bored of staying at home, so I said okay.'

They caught up with him. 'Hello Jaswinder-ji,' greeted Raghuraman. 'How's work?'

'Not bad, Raghu-ji, I can't tell you how glad I'm to see you today. Are you feeling better?'

'Yes. Wanted a change. Otherwise Padma, poor girl, will cook something for me in the morning before leaving for work.'

'You'll be fine, Raghu-ji. If you need any help, you can call me and our other friends too. We are all there,' assured Jaswinder, sitting with them.

There were other Fellows who greeted Raghuraman. The three Tamil men sat at a corner table with Sunil Yadav. Lunch over, Padma went to the Mess Manager to pay for the month. Then she waited with Jaswinder, looking for Raghuraman. The three Tamil men and Yadav were talking to him. He gestured to them to go ahead, and waved the key of their flat to Padma to say he has it. The two women left for the Institute.

After about an hour, Padma went to the reception, called home to assure herself that Raghuraman had reached and was resting. She returned to the large table and resumed her work. Today is one of my better days, she told herself. It's not just the information and source materials I've garnered. I'm also getting flashes of ideas that I'm itching to include in my draft. For a few minutes she pondered if she should continue her work in the library or go home and write. She opted for the second, picked up her shoulder bag and her handbag and left for her flat.

'Leaving early?' asked the receptionist. 'All well at home?'

'All well, Mrs Sharma. Thanks so much. Just want to write my stuff,' she smiled on her way out.

Raghuraman was surprised to see her back early, but was pleased when she said she was going to write.

'Let me make the tea today,' he offered. 'Wash up and settle down to write.'

Padma joined him in the balcony. Over tea he said, 'Don't cook, Padma. I'll make cheese-tomato sandwich toast for dinner. We'll have fruits and the flavoured yoghurt we got from the mall.'

Padma settled down at her desk, relieved to see Raghuraman eager and happy to make his favourite cheese-tomato sandwich toast. For the next two hours, she was at the mercy of her thoughts that stormed inside her mind with a speed that spiralled out of control. Her hands went numb with the strain of writing. She clenched and unclenched her fingers, stretched out her arms and did some shoulder exercises. The wholesome aroma of cheese-tomato toast floated from the kitchen. Padma went in to find Raghuraman making the last of the toast with the sandwich toaster. She washed her hands and set the table for their dinner. She put out tomato and green chilli sauce to go with the toast, put out fruits, flavoured yoghurt, bottles of water and waited.

'All done,' beamed Raghuraman, bringing a covered pile of hot cheese-tomato sandwich toast to the table.

'Yummy, Raghu!' smiled Padma, getting up to hug his shoulders from behind. 'Stay well. Enjoy the ambience of Shimla before we return to dusty, hot Delhi.'

Ah, the toast was such a welcome change from rice and *rotis*. They ate their bowls of freshly cut fruits and licked off the last bit of flavoured yoghurt from the packs. Padma got up to clear the table.

'Padma, sit for a while. We can clear the table later. First listen to me. I want to alert you about something. It's important,' said Raghuraman.

'Why, what happened?'

'You know, after you left the three men from Tamil Nadu surrounded me,' said Raghuraman.

'I saw that. One of them called you a very nice man,' said Padma.

'You'll soon find out why,' he smiled. 'They've been tailing me for about a week, relentlessly.'

Padma laughed. 'They tail me too, whenever they get a chance to. I guess they're happy to find two people in the hills who can talk to them in Tamil.'

'No! There's a deeper reason. Thittakudi, Namakkal and Chengalpattu…'

Padma laughed aloud. 'For God's sake, Raghu, they have names!'

'Never mind. I get confused about their names. For now, their places, their *ooru*, will do. Coming to the point, all three of them have been trying to make friends with me in the fond hope that we'll invite them for dinner someday soon.'

'What!'

'Yes! According to their opinion poll, I'm the luckiest man on this campus. When I asked them why, they said, "Sir, Madam gives you *idli, dosa, utthappam* with *sambar* and *chutney*, that's why you don't come to the Mess again for dinner." And this, despite my telling them so many times that I keep poor health, that I can't even eat normal food on many days. Imagine!'

'And still they expect a feast?' asked Padma, incredulous. 'Oh my God! Make *idli, dosa* and *utthappam*, sitting on top of these hills? And who'll do the grinding for the batter, pray? And prepare all those things on a small stove?'

'Madam Dr Padma Raghuraman, who else?' said Raghu, his lips curling in sarcasm. 'The appointed Fellow of IIAS, who will now go hunting around for logs of wood to start a big fire crackling in this kitchen on the hills. Over the blazing fire, she'll place a large pot to make *sambar*, she'll grind rice and *urad dal* for the batter for a little over an hour. After all, that's what you're here for, didn't you know? So, do you want to gather logs of wood or may be go buy a new gas range with a double stove, just so that they can have *idli, dosa, utthappam* and so on…?' he asked.

'Like hell! How do they even expect that I would spend two hours slogging to cook for them? Preposterous!' fumed Padma, her face flushed in anger.

'Padma, I warn you. Seriously! If you give them just an inch, they'll eat you out of the house. I told them point blank that we only have bread every night as you're under pressure to complete your work within a stipulated period of time. Just avoid them.'

***

Jaswinder and Padma walked towards the Mess. Raghuraman had reached the Mess ahead of them. He waved at them to say that he has reserved places for them on the table. The two women filled their plates and sat down with him. Padma glanced at the corner table where the three Tamil men sat with Sunil Yadav.

'There they are, Namakkal, Chengalpattu and Thittakudi,' said Raghu.

'Are they all surnames?' asked Jaswinder. 'I thought one of them was called Murugesan, and the others… I forget…'

Raghu laughed. 'Jaswinder-ji, I mentioned the places they come from so that we'll remember them more vividly. Padma, do you know what that guy Sunil Yadav told me just before the three men joined him?'

'Tell me.'

'He said according to their latest opinion poll, I must be the unluckiest Tamil man on the campus.'

'What!'

'Want to know why? It's because my wife gives me bread for dinner. "In our home town, only dogs eat bread," they told Yadav, it seems.'

Jaswinder burst out laughing. She had a problem controlling her laughter. Padma joined in, aware that many heads turned towards them from other tables while Namakkal, Chengalpattu, Thittakudi and Yadav gave them a startled look.

FLOATING FREE

Harshavardhini sat on the swing, a still, motionless figure. The birds were still around, for it was not too late in the evening. After the revelry and the din of an entire day spent at Disneyland Resort, Harshavardhini needed the quiet space of this community park at Irvine, California. Her friends pulled her into one last trip to the Resort before she would leave Anaheim in Orange County for Delhi. She spent the day taking thrilling rides, watching shows, shaking hands with a friendly Mickey Mouse, eating endlessly, winning games and losing, all the time looking at things through the eyes of her children. She longed for their company. They would have doubled her joy.

Perched on the swing, she looked at the children playing around in the park under the watchful eyes of their parents. On the lanes around the edge of the park, people were walking briskly, some were jogging at a steady pace. Harshi, as she was called by most of her family and friends, counted the remaining days she had in Irvine, before she would take her flight back to home in Delhi, four days from now. 'I should come to this park again before I leave', she told herself, pushing the uncomfortable thoughts away about tidying up the apartment before handing it over and packing clothes, books and things from the final shopping trip.

She would miss Susan Green, who had not only enrolled for the same course, but also shared Harshi's nice apartment on the campus. Susan offered to share the rent and both of them could put the money saved to good use. They each had a room of their own and met only in the living room, the kitchen and dining room in that comfortable, sunny and spacious two-bedroom apartment. Sure enough, Susan spelt her name as Hershey, after the famous chocolate in the US and justified it by saying it sounds the same as 'Harshi'. She became Hershey to everybody else in her course, including the professors. It was a happy surprise to find that Susan was equally earnest in giving her full focus to this rare course on hermeneutics, for which the university had hand-picked a galaxy of faculty from the rest of the US—some of the best minds from Princeton, Harvard, Berkeley, Stanford, Yale and Chicago and a culturally diverse bunch of participants both American and from overseas, whose paper publications were the main criteria for selection.

Before the programme started, Susan, Harshi and the others were in awe of the professors and their fame. All of them were star academics whose books they had read and admired in print, and who had influenced their methods of teaching and thinking. Now they were going to see them in flesh and hear them. What would they look like? And their voice, would it touch them?

The professors arrived like a proverbial breath of fresh air and put them through a breathless pace of course work. Susan, Harshi and most of the others loved it, every moment of it.

Harshi bought some of the books written by these academics, got them inscribed by the authors and sent them home by surface mail, as most of the books were heavy hardback editions. It was unlikely that she would find them in the bookshops in Delhi. Now she was left with only a few light paperbacks to pack along with her clothes and the shopping she had done for Siddharth, her husband, and their children. She was anxious to return home and relieve him of all the additional work he had taken on. It was so brave of him to take care of their kids and home in her absence.

If only her mother had been around, she would've been the first one to reach their home to take complete charge of running the house and managing the kids who got along with her very well. But Amma left this world and for the first time in their lives, Siddharth and Harshi had to manage their travels out of the country and other professional contingencies without her. It was tough. As they struggled hard to cope with their work, home and kids, they realized how much Amma had taken upon herself selflessly, to let the two of them function peacefully. Harshi couldn't have gotten her PhD, made some significant career moves, pursued creative writing and taken Indian writing to other parts of the world without her. Thanks to Amma, both Siddharth and Harshi could be away from home with a sense of security that their children were looked after by their doting grandmother.

Now, there was the reality of the next few days. The apartment had to be thoroughly cleaned before she handed it over, and there was the packing.

Let me not think of that, let me just listen to the restful sounds of this evening, thought Harshi, closing her eyes. She continued to sit still on the swing when she heard a faint buzz near her face. Oh God, that is probably a honeybee! It would surely sting! Slowly, she opened her eyes to avert the bee. It was a hummingbird fluttering its delicate wings that had caused the sustained drone. It now hovered very close to her face, almost making eye contact with her. It can't harm me, I'm wearing my specs, that'll protect my eyes. Rather, I shouldn't harm this darling little bird by my hard stare. Let me just pretend that it's not there, even though it's hovering near my nose now. Let me not scare it away by my jerky movements. I'll sit absolutely still and just listen.

Harshi froze like a statue. This dainty little bird with tiny feet, it doesn't seem to sit anywhere to rest, but just hovers around so joyfully. It's blowing gusts of happiness on my face with its small wings. It's telling me something.

She closed her eyes to absorb the beauty of the moment. It was in California that she got to see the famed humming birds for the first time. It was also interesting to read about them. She recalled a mythical lore that was wrapped around this bird. The lines came across as sheer poetry!

Legends say that hummingbirds float free of time, carrying our hopes for love, joy and celebration. The hummingbird's delicate grace reminds us that life is rich, beauty is everywhere, every personal connection has meaning and that laughter is life's sweetest creation.

Slowly, Harshi opened her eyes. The bird flew away from her, made a large arc to hover over the flowering plants nearby, and then returned to circle around her face. It moved close to her ears and was saying something with its flapping wings. Harshi nodded.

'I know, little bird. I know you're my Amma who has come back from the other world to talk to me for a while,' whispered Harshi, her eyes going moist. Amma, I know this is you, flapping within the tender little body of this humming bird. Yes, I hear you clearly. You're my fragile, underweight Amma with innumerable health issues that were unmatched with your immense reserves of strength.

'A hummingbird being small, it is logical that its egg is also small—it is just the size of a pea,' said an article in *National Geographic*. But Amma, to everybody's shock, you gave birth to me, an overweight baby, by normal delivery! The doctors and the family found it miraculous that a thin, emaciated, undernourished, underweight young woman like you, who never kept well for long, would deliver a baby like me. You told me that the newborn baby dresses that were made for me wouldn't fit, that new dresses were ordered and that there was a permanent mark of black kohl on my left cheek close to my ear that my grandma had applied, to remove *kann drishti*.

You raised me without a nanny, although I gave you a tough time. I was naughty, adventurous, but you saw me through all that and more, and those were my forays into sports and athletics. You never once forgot to alert me that I shouldn't slacken in my studies. Your frequent spells of illness, your inability to eat, or retain anything you eat, cast a shadow on our lives. You continued to lose weight, yet your unconditional love for me and for your family throbbed on your little feathered bird breast.

You gave me a baby brother at great cost to your life and health. The doctors were amazed to note your high pain threshold. My grandparents were furious that you should have risked your life with another pregnancy, but you pacified them by saying your husband and in-laws craved for a male child.

When the doctors diagnosed a serious malfunction in your small intestine, you had to go through a surgery. I was in primary school then. I would rush to the hospital as soon as I returned from school and you sat up on bed to butter those long, crisp golden-hued imported biscuits for me to eat. Eyes shining, you would ask me about my day and if I had played games after school. As if on cue, you would apply butter on one more biscuit and put it on my plate…and one more, and one more…until I couldn't eat any more.

Post-surgery, the doctors put you on a liquid diet that was to continue for the next 15 years! Naturally, you lost more weight and became this frail packet of indefatigable energy, love and selflessness that astonished all of us. Still, there were some cruel people in our extended family who took you for granted. I seethed with anger, one of the many other spells of anger I was to experience as a growing girl child. Later, I had to learn a lot about anger management, as did my friends. Some of my anger was directed against you as well. 'You've internalised patriarchy and that's regressive!' I would argue hotly, while you looked bewildered by my feminist pedagogy, a new burden I carry now, along with my peers. We fought over issues, like mothers and daughters do, until I realised that you too were quietly evolving as a clever feminist-in-the-making, unbeknown to the family. Wisely, you didn't squander any feminist vocabulary on the resistant family. Instead, you used strategies to grow your wings independently, right under their nose!

What blossomed through all these travails was your astonishing talent for painting. You were a natural! Noting this, my grandfather enrolled you in a professional course on painting in a Fine Arts College. He ordered for the branded imported paints, Windsor & Newton, that were specially flown all the way from England. Their superior quality glows till date in the rich tints behind the glass of your framed paintings. While your diet was liquid, your output was solid. In a prolific abundance, you did landscapes, still-life, thematic triptychs and stunning portraits that won accolades from your teachers and art critics for their intuitive depth. The water colours, charcoal sketches and oil on canvas drew the attention of visitors in art galleries. Your high point was portraiture. You were counted as one of the best artists for your haunting portraits of well-known personalities such as Sri Aurobindo, Sri Ramakrishna Paramahans, his consort Sarada Devi and the lovely Shobhana Samarth. As for Mahatma Gandhi, commissions rained on you for painting his portraits. Art critics were quick to observe that you excelled especially in portraits of elderly people, and made the wrinkles on their face speak eloquently of all they had endured in life. Portraits became your USP, your Unique Selling Proposition. To everybody's utter surprise, you chose to paint me. Why me, a mere frisky 10-year old, an odd misfit in this gallery of the famous? I sat for you, thrilled beyond belief, while you chided me for fidgeting on my chair. When an artist, a scion of the Tagore family visited our home to buy two of your paintings, you sat demurely in a far corner with a shy smile on your face, and let my father completely monopolise the conversation with the distinguished gentleman.

Amma, you were here, there, everywhere, flying around, looking after us and the large extended family selflessly. You were like seven women put together. And when you left, all seven of you went out of our lives on a single day. The world around me shrank to a miserable little size. Something vital went out of my life. And now Amma, you're back in the body of this small hummingbird that just doesn't let me go out of its orbit. Like this bird with its tiny legs, you with your small fragile frame, were a strong woman. Ephemeral, yet eternal. You float on time, so I will always wait for you. You'll come when I need you, I know. You're untrammeled by body mass or messy emotions that weigh us down. You lived life the simple way—with love, joy, service and acceptance.

The bird went on humming near Harshi's ears.

GUILT TRIP

Pratibha, her cousin Shashi and their Tamil friend Indira set off from their hostel in Maharani Arts & Science College to the nearest bus station. They had packed their things into one small stroller suitcase for their trip to Srirangapatna, which was a short bus ride from Mysore. Each one of them had a large backpack into which they stuffed two sets of *salwar* suits, spare inner wear, head scarves, towels, toilet soap and other essentials such as sandwiches, biscuits, fruits and water bottles. Pratibha, the natural 'leader' had thoughtfully taken three large plastic bags to carry their drenched *salwar* suits after their bath in the river Kaveri. They couldn't contain their excitement, most of which stemmed from the fact that it was a secret trip, undisclosed to their parents who would have descended on them like a ton of bricks to dissuade them from travelling unescorted. The families knew each other, all the more reason to keep it a secret.

Typically, the families would have assured their girls that they would certainly take them to Srirangapatna at the earliest opportunity, show them around the town, and couldn't they wait please? This is after all, their very first year in Mysore and they had just started off as first year students of the college. But the girls wanted to go on their own, because they had another undisclosed plan in Srirangapatna, which would have certainly made their families swoop down on them in fury.

***

The bus wasn't crowded. By the time they settled in their seats, had their sandwiches, bought tea from vendors, they were nearing Srirangapatna. Some passengers looked like they were travelling mainly to see the famous Sri Ranganathaswamy temple.

'See there, you can see the top of the temple *gopuram*,' said Indira, bowing her head in the temple's direction, her hands pressed together.

'You must've been there?' asked Shashi.

'Several times! How can I not visit the temple of Ranganathaswamy? He is our family deity!' replied Indira.

'Of course! More so because you're an Iyengar from Hebbar,' remarked Pratibha.

'Hebbar or not, an Iyengar from anywhere will make it a point to visit! So will Iyers, I bet,' said Indira, bowing down her head again.

The bus stopped at Srirangapatna. The girls hoisted their backpacks, adjusted the straps on their shoulders and took their small suitcase from the luggage rack. They went to a taxi stand. Pratibha spoke to a man in Kannada, 'Take us to the nearest point to river Kaveri from here.'

'Very well, *ammauvare*. Come,' he said, offering to keep the suitcase in the boot.

'No need,' said Pratibha. 'Let it be with us or we'll forget it.'

The man got in and said, 'Come on all of you. Say aloud, Devi Kaveriamma, here we come, your devotees!' he urged them. The girls chorused loudly in Kannada, 'Devi Kaveriamma, here we come, your daughters and devotees!' He nodded and cheered them, and started the taxi.

The next minute they broke off in English and took a pledge of secrecy that none of them would ever divulge their trip taken specially to bathe in the river Kaveri.

***

On reaching the river bank, they inquired about the area marked off for bathers and walked toward it. Some bathers were already splashing around happily, letting the river water swirl around them. They were revellers who obviously enjoyed the touch of the flowing river wrapping around their bodies. Most of them were shoulder deep in the water, while the braver ones allowed the water to reach up to their neck, scooping it up to splash on their faces. A few devout ones folded their hands in reverence for goddess Kaveri, and prayed with their eyes closed. Indira, the Tamil friend of the two Kannada girls Pratibha and Shashi, recalled how she was brought up to believe that the river Kaveri is a personification of a divine, life-giving mother who nourished the lands of Tamil Nadu and Karnataka and made them fertile.

The three young women rolled up the lower end of their *salwar*s and gingerly stepped into the river. Instantly as it were, they pulled back their feet.

'Brr! The water is so cold!' Shashi exclaimed.

'And it's also flowing so rapidly, we may be carried away by the strong current. Careful, Shashi, step back!' warned her worried cousin, Pratibha.

The bathers glanced at the three young women and resumed splashing about happily in the river water. How fearless they looked. Some had ventured deeper inside. Just look at their confidence, thought Indira, staring at them at them enviously.

'It's all our fault,' declared Indira. 'We should've learnt swimming despite our family's objections. That would've made us shed the fear of water.'

'Yes. And now, I've the additional responsibility of looking after Shashi.' Shashi was younger than Pratibha by a year. 'Ever since we joined Maharani College, my parents and hers look up to me as her guardian. Hey Shashi, you better listen to me!'

The younger girl grinned and brought her hand to her head in a salute.

'Both our families are hand in glove with each other to prevent us from going anywhere near the river.'

'It's only when we were planning to make this little trip to the river that I realised we have a common factor that binds all of us,' smiled Indira.

'And that is?' Shashi asked.

'None of us can swim. I was effectively prevented by my family from taking swimming lessons when every second girl I know has learnt swimming,' said Indira, her face flushing in anger.

'Never mind,' said Pratibha. 'Let's try to bathe in an area that has shallow waters. When we return home this time, we'll seriously find out the possibility of enrolling for swimming lessons.'

'Learn swimming at this age?' asked Shashi.

'Why ever not?' retorted Indira. 'Let's google and find out if there are special swimming lessons for young women above 20.'

'Oh, there must be!' said Pratibha. 'You know Indira, in our family it seems there was an unfortunate instance of someone who drowned at the age of 18. That too in a swimming pool. That was his very first day at a club to learn swimming. Our families were so shattered by this tragic happening that they went into an astrology mode! They got his horoscope analysed by three astrologers. All of them declared that he was destined to die by water and went further to say that according to the astrological indication, there could be a danger from water for others in the family too. "Please don't step into any river or ocean. Don't learn swimming. Do anything else you want to", the family pleaded. They looked so scared that we complied with their warning. Wish we hadn't', she rued, adding, 'now, they've become intensely hydrophobic.'

'As for me, I missed every opportunity to learn swimming while at school,' said Indira. 'Later, when I tried to enrol for swimming lessons, my family discouraged me saying I'm too old to learn. They argued that the best age to learn is when one is a child. To tell you the truth, even I became diffident. The older I grew, the more scared I got of water. Now all I can boast of is standing on the fringe of the ocean in Marina Beach in Chennai and let the frothy waters of the waves bathe my legs.'

They became aware of curious eyes looking at them as they stood hesitantly on the dry river bed. It was embarrassing. They looked around to see if anyone could be identified as a local to consult for a safer area for bathing, especially for people who cannot swim. They found a boy in shorts and a faded T-shirt.

Pratibha asked him in Kannada if he lived in Srirangapatna. He nodded. When she told him about their requirement, he pointed at a direction and said, 'Walk for about a kilometre from here, and you'll find an open space. Kaveriamma thins out at that place. You can easily bathe in that area without any fear,' he smiled.

They trudged in the direction he pointed and reached a spot that was at a distance from the adventurous swimmers and bathers. They reached a clearing with an open space under the sky on the left side of the river. At the far end of the clearing, a cluster of trees and dense bushes bordered the area and gave them a sense of privacy. The girls felt less shy and there were only a few bathers and swimmers. Like the boy said, the river did seem to be thinner, so it looked less threatening to them. They rolled up their *salwar*s again and stepped into the waters.

'Oh, the water is equally cold here,' said Pratibha, shivering.

'It's river water, after all,' said Shashi.

'The waters in Marina beach are not this cold. In fact, they have a comfortable warmth even in the evening,' said Indira.

'The water is flowing so rapidly… makes me wary of stepping in,' said Pratibha. 'What if it carries away all three of us in its flow? Shashi! Come back at once,' she said, raising her voice.

'Shh! Softly. Even here, some of these bathers are looking at us hesitating and scratching our heads.'

'True. What a shame! They must be laughing at us, a bunch of cowards. Let alone swim, we're not even bathing.'

'I do sense their eyes on us. Let's walk a little farther. They can't see us clearly from there.'

'Yes, there are only a few bathers there. Come, pick up your backpacks and we'll move on to that secluded spot.'

Indira pulled the small stroller suitcase.

Now this stretch had privacy. They stepped into the water again, gritting their teeth against the cold. They scooped up water in their hands and let it dribble down their neck and shoulders.

'Strange, not one of us thought of bringing mugs to scoop out water and pour it on ourselves.'

'After the initial shock, we'll get used to the coldness of the water,' said Shashi.

'You're right! I'm enjoying the cold water now. It looks so clean, so clear,' said Pratibha.

They looked at each other and laughed at the way they were bathing their face and arms part by part, instead of immersing themselves in the waters.

They washed their face and hands and then stepped on to the shore to look at the gurgling, swirling waters in the serene environment. They dried their feet, ankles and calves and rolled down their *salwar*s. They brushed their hair, tidied up and wrapped scarves around their heads against the strong wind that blew around them.

'The good news is we don't have to change our *salwars*,' said Indira.

The girls nodded.

'Bhagyalakshmi!'

They looked around and then turned their eyes toward the few people who were bathing in the middle of the river. Who called out so loudly? The bathers were calmly splashing about. So Bhagyalakshmi couldn't be from their group. Then where is she and who called out in such a booming voice? They peered at the group of bathers who looked unperturbed. Who is this girl Bhagyalakshmi?

The thick foliage of the bushes in the distance rustled a bit. Then it parted to show something grey, flapping its ears. The three friends watched, their eyes transfixed when they saw a baby elephant emerging from the thicket between the trees, with its mahout running behind in hot pursuit.

'Bhagyalakshmi, stop! Stop this minute!' said the mahout angrily, cracking the whip in his hand that sliced the air to make a sharp swishing sound.

Baby Bhagyalakshmi turned her head once to look at him and shook her head sideways in a frolicsome way. And then she started running toward the three young women.

'Oh no!' screamed Pratibha, petrified. 'This baby elephant is heading straight toward us. Quick, pick up your backpacks. Let's run!'

'Bhagya!' shouted the mahout. 'Stop running, this minute! Your mother has been looking for you. She would be worried to see you missing,' he scolded in Kannada.

She shook her head again playfully and kept running toward the three women.

'I say Bhagyalakshmi, stop or else!' cried the mahout, tossing the switch twice in the air to make a crackling sound.

Suddenly, Bhagyalakshmi stopped. She stood for a moment looking at the flowing waters of Kaveri. Abruptly, she changed her direction and ran toward the river.

'No Bhagya, stop! Listen!'

'Thank God,' said Shashi, relieved to see the baby elephant targeting the river instead of running towards them.

Bhagyalakshmi plunged into the waters with a big splash. The three of them looked on, fascinated by the way she was sloshing about merrily. She dipped her head inside the river till she was completely immersed, and they could only see a small portion of the curved top of her grey head above the water.

'Oh god, what has happened? Is she drowning?' asked Shashi, very alarmed. The mahout stood watching, and this time a broad smile spread over his swarthy face. The few bathers around the waters laughed and carried on fearlessly, not one bit disturbed that a baby elephant had joined them in the waters.

'Naughty girl! Wait till I report this to your mother. She'll give you a beating with her long trunk,' scolded the mahout, still laughing at baby Bhagya's playful antics in water.

The three women relaxed and watched, eyes riveted on the baby elephant. She dipped her head again into the waters and then lifted her head to squirt water in a straight jet directly at the three girls on the river bank. Utterly shocked, the girls stepped back.

'Hey, Bhagya, what are you doing, you silly girl? I say stop!' said the mahout, very angry at the way she repeatedly dipped her trunk to suck in water, and then squirt, targeting the girls. Bhagya seemed to be delighted to see the shock on their face. The mahout looked at the girls who stood rooted on the spot, as if they were under some spell and couldn't move away from Bhagya's range. Their clothes were completely drenched.

Hesitantly, he approached the girls. Pressing his hands together, he apologised in Kannada, '*Ammauvre*! I'm so sorry! Very sorry,' he pleaded. 'Bhagyalakshmi is such a naughty little girl, very difficult to handle. See, how she doesn't obey even me? Doesn't listen to her mother either. Hey Bhagya, wait till I take you to your mother, and then we'll see,' he warned, whirling his switch in the air in a circular motion that now echoed with sharp sounds.

'It's all right,' said Shashi. 'Don't worry. After all, we came to bathe in the river.'

'But you've already bathed and changed into dry clothes and now, this mischievous girl...Hey Bhagya!' he turned around to warn her again, then resumed his apology. '*Ammauvre*, see how she is. I tried my best to stop her but she is very wilful. Gives me a lot of trouble all day long.'

The mahout stood there, arms folded, the switch tucked into his elbow, as he watched Bhagya, flapping her large ears in the water. She was loath to come out. Snatching this moment, the three girls quickly gathered their backpacks, the suitcase and the damp towels and moved away to a spot from where they could still see Bhagya.

At last she emerged from the water having had her fill of fun and now stood calmly beside her mahout who was showering her with fond endearments, 'Our little princess. She not only bathed in the sacred waters of Kaveri, she also gave a second bath to the three ladies. They're so nice, they've forgiven you. Mischievous girl!'

She snuggled up close to him, her body brushing his as she walked.

'My darling little princess. I'll tell your great mother about your naughty pranks today. Won't she be proud of her little girl?'

Bhagya shook her head, pointed her trunk upwards and then curled it around his arms. He stroked her back and her face.

'Come now. Time for you to eat and cuddle up with your mother. I've the juiciest sugar cane for both of you,' said the mahout.

Indira smiled at the retreating figure. 'Bhagya!' she called, softly.

'Oh no, don't call her!' cautioned Pratibha. 'She'll come back running and splash water on us all over again. Come, let's go back to the bus station and change our damp clothes in the washroom. We'll stuff them into the big plastic bags'

'Hope the taxi driver lets us get in,' said Indira.

'We'll tell him we bathed in the river, Ha, ha! It's half true, isn't it? We did have a bath in the river water,' laughed Shashi.

'We have to thank Bhagya for that. Whew! What an experience!' said Pratibha.

'Unforgettable,' said Indira.

'But remember our pledge?' said Pratibha. 'Not a word to our families!'

'Of course! If they get to know, we lose their trust, forever,' said Indira.

They laughed as they shivered, turning back to take another look at the silver waters of Kaveri glistening in the sunlight. They looked at the thicket and the foliage of the forested area. It seemed to have closed like a curtain after Bhagya's splendid performance.

It was a middle-aged driver this time. He opened the door of his taxi, waving aside their apologies for their wet clothes.

'Never mind. Had a good bath, with the blessings of Kaveriamma? Never mind. Lots of tourists come to my taxi with wet clothes. It's a *punya sthal*, after all.'

THE COLOUR GREEN

Vibha Kaushik walked slowly, turning back every two minutes to check if Ramya could be spotted on the same road. She stopped for a minute to send her another message on her phone and then resumed walking.

There was a blip. A message from Ramya: Vibha, sorry I can't join you for a walk. I'm too tired. Cooked for 10 dinner guests yesterday.

Vibha darted off a reply: Oh God! Take care, dear. Just rest.

Cooked for 10 dinner guests? At this age? I'm about the same age as Ramya. Thankfully, whenever we come to the US, Sandeep helps me with cooking, dish-washing, laundry, the whole works. Ramya has come alone this time, having lost Seshadri, her husband. Vibha walked on, glancing at the maple trees dripping with the lush colours of the fall season in this part of California. It was interesting the way orange, copper, yellow and rust red vied with the still green leaves in the splash of hues. I must capture these rich tints while I'm still here, thought Vibha, clicking a few pictures with her phone. Then she turned around and walked briskly toward her daughter Mrinalini's home, reminding herself of the breakfast and meals she had to prepare.

Mrinalini and Sudhir, her son-in-law, had wanted *poha* for breakfast. On reaching home, she soaked the flattened rice, chopped vegetables, ginger and green chillies, sautéed all of them with the drained rice and garnished it with lemon juice. *Poha* done, she scooped it up in a bowl, covered and placed it on the dining table. Next, she got busy making scrambled eggs for her grandkids. She peeped into the living room to say, 'Sandeep, have *poha* while it's hot. I'm going for a shower,' and went to the washroom.

After bath and prayers, Vibha had her share of *poha*. Mrinalini and Sudhir had eaten *poha*, packed yesterday's dinner for their lunch in office and left for work. The children had left for school. Now she had to cook for lunch and make some extra dishes for dinner. She took out frozen peas to make the green peas and potato curry with a tomato gravy that they liked very much. From the fridge, she took out carrots and string beans. Sandeep was already at the table, ready with the chopping board. He sat down and chopped them fine.

'The *poha* was very nice,' he smiled. Her eyes lingered on him for a moment. Back home in Delhi, Sandeep didn't have to chop vegetables. They had a cook and a domestic help who did a lot of background work. Both Sandeep and Vibha had retired from active government service as senior officers in the Income Tax and the Audit and Accounts departments respectively. That's how they had met, while training at the Academy as IRS officers after cracking their civil service exams. It had been a nice journey together. Vibha had warmed up to him because he was one of the few gender-neutral officers who carried no excess baggage or prejudice. They got married, had a good life, a steady career and had retired, looking forward to doing other things that they hadn't found the time for earlier. One such activity was their *Gita* class held at Chinmaya Mission. The more they listened to discourses on *Gita*, the more they got immersed in studying the recommended books.

'Anything else to be chopped?' asked Sandeep.

'Aah…I'll make okra. They have to be split without cutting them altogether,' said Vibha.

'I'll manage that. I've seen the way you do it,' said Sandeep, splitting them neatly in the center.

'We haven't found any time to study for our *Gita* class. Tonight, I'm going to talk to Mrinalini,' said Sandeep.

'About what?'

'Well, I'm going to ask her why she leaves the cooking entirely to you the minute we enter this house. Doesn't she do any cooking all the year round when we're not here?'

'I'm not so sure we should raise the issue.'

'Why ever not, Vibha? You do a lot of customized cooking for her whenever they come over to Delhi, despite having a cook. All the while Mrinalini has a good time shopping, visiting friends and showing places to her children like it's a Bharat Darshan tour by India Tourism Inc. Then you do all the cooking whenever you come here. You've retired, just like I have. Does she need any more proof that we've aged, and we can't work like before?'

'Doesn't ever seem to strike her,' murmured Vibha, joining him in splitting okra.

'So, we'll din it into her head,' said Sandeep.

'You know why Ramya couldn't join me for the morning walk today?'

'What happened?'

'Her son had invited 10 dinner guests last night. She just didn't have the strength to get up from her bed.'

'That is atrocious!'

'To say the least. Her daughter-in-law doesn't lift her little finger to help. As for her son, the less said, the better. He is spineless and very scared of his wife. I feel sorry for Ramya. Since Seshadri passed on, she has come alone in answer to her son's invitation, and promptly got trapped in his hidden agenda—the endless cooking and house work.'

Sandeep was silently splitting the okra.

'Sandeep, you help me so much with cooking and laundry. And I've you to share my thoughts. Poor Ramya, she has come alone this time.'

'I know. I'm mentally tired of all this charade our children are playing, and the way we too play along with them,' said Sandeep, the frown deepening on his face. 'I've been seeing this ritual of going to USA to be with our children and then returning home every time with bitter thoughts about how our grown-up sons and daughters have become so monstrously selfish.'

'And self-centered,' said Vibha. 'At times I think we're equally to be blamed, to make this visit as some kind of an annual pilgrimage, slave in their household, and then slave again for them when they visit us with their kids.'

'That's what I said. Go and meet Ramya someday soon. She needs someone to talk to.'

'Oh, the last time I went over to her place, it was a terrible sight. She was talking to me while something was on the griddle on one gas burner, and something else simmering in a vessel on the other. All the while, her hands were going up and down, reaching for spices or some ingredient on the shelf just above the gas range. Either she is cooking, loading-unloading the dishwasher unendingly, doing laundry, grinding batter for *idli*, or she is taken to the super market for buying grocery, vegetables and fruits for the same grind the next week. All in much the same way as we're doing here. The only difference is she is alone this time.'

Sandeep got up and went to the garage to check the laundry.

In the kitchen, Vibha kneaded the flour for *chapattis*, wrapped the dough with a damp cloth and kept it inside a covered vessel. She went to the garage, took the pile of washed clothes to the backyard, put them out on the washing line and came in. 'Want some tea?' she called out.

'Come on here,' said Sandeep, from their room.

She wiped her hands in a towel and went in to see Sandeep smiling over a tray, all laid out. The tea cosy was pulled snugly over the pot.

'Aah!' said Vibha, sinking into a lounge chair. 'Thanks, Sandeep. Just the thing we need, before we study a bit for our *Gita* class.'

In Chinmaya Mission, they met a nice set of people who were quite earnest in learning about Sri Krishna's doctrine of *karma* and the complications it got people into. The Mission organized *Gita* discourses by inviting many erudite speakers from other Chinmaya centers worldwide. The Q&A sessions were especially lively. Each person defined *karma* according to his/her life and justified actions based on circumstances. The more they dug, the deeper the possibilities that opened up for them. With time it grew on them, the belief that one could get a deep sense of satisfaction and fulfillment if one had done what we term as 'duty' or *karma*—to one's parents, spouses, children, the organisations one worked for, one's country and so on.

They met Ramya Seshadri in their *Gita* class. A doctor with the Apollo Hospitals, she had retired recently after clocking several years of service. Now she was planning to get a placement as a consultant with a few accredited clinics. She said her husband was suffering from Parkinson's disease and impaired movements. His speech was also getting slurred. When she didn't attend classes for some time, they thought she was busy attending on her husband. Ramya returned after a long absence and told them quietly that her husband had passed on, there were ceremonies and her house was swarming with relatives. She said she didn't know which was her dominant emotion—her shock and grief over losing her husband, or her relief that he was at last liberated from his wasted body and would find a new one now in his next birth. Vibha and Sandeep admired her courage and wondered if the systematic study of *Gita*, and her conditioning as a doctor had something to do with her fortitude and equanimity.

Ramya's son Rajiv and daughter-in-law Chitra had come over with their children for the obsequies. That over, Rajiv said, 'This has been a shock for you Amma, you need a break. You couldn't come to California all these years because of Appa's condition. Now come over as soon as you can.'

'But I'm waiting for some clinics to revert to my application,' she protested.

'I'm sure that will take a while, Amma. You can always fly back as soon as you hear from them,' said Rajiv.

She saw his point and agreed to follow Rajiv a little later.

***

And she had walked straight into their hidden agenda—a dreary regimentation of cooking, cleaning, loading/unloading the dishwasher, laundry and shopping for grocery, vegetables, fruits and other odd things. After having struggled with Seshadri's illness for years on end, after all the tension, uncertainty and the emotional exhaustion of having done more than her best only to lose him in the end, she was now tired beyond belief. She missed Savitri, her cook back home, and the friendly chats she had with her. Savitri's face would light up whenever Ramya bought books, stationery and school uniforms for her children. She was a great comfort and companion to Ramya after Seshadri had passed on. How she would gently coax her to eat her meals when she was totally off food. A genuinely compassionate soul, as compared to Ramya's visiting family that offered just lip sympathy.

***

'I've an idea, Vibha,' said Sandeep, sipping his tea.

'Before you tell me, I want to say how much I enjoyed this *elaichi* tea,' said Vibha, pouring out two more cups for themselves.

'Pleasure, Madam,' he laughed, with a flourish of his arm. 'My idea is simple. Let me come with you on your morning walk tomorrow, that is, if Ramya-ji also agrees to come. Then we could both talk to her, comfort her.'

'I already got a message that she'll join me for a walk tomorrow. I think she badly needs to talk, and that's the only private moment we get. Do join us, Sandeep. We'll take a walk and find a nice garden seat somewhere to sit down and chat.'

'Done.'

***

Vibha recalled her chat with Ramya the last time they walked together. They talked about the change that had come over their NRI children in the US. They had discussed, although half in jest, if it had something to do with the colour green, as in dollar bills—'it's a wicked colour, a sick colour, the colour of a monster', they had argued, hotly. The colour green had lured their children away from the shores of India, but that was okay. Their children wanted success, recognition, affluence and a good lifestyle. That was really okay. But it had also brought about an alarming change in them over a period of time. They had come to look upon their visiting mothers, mothers-in-law, sisters and aunts as cooks, maids, nannies and caretakers of their house. Never mind if the mothers are educated, qualified professionals who had worked very hard in their chosen field, had grown older and retired and were now visiting them only for a holiday.

Vibha took the tray to the kitchen, washed the set and returned to their room to study. Sandeep was already poring over a book.

***

It was Ramya who had walked ahead of them the following morning. She waved at them and smiled when she spotted them.

'Good morning Sandeep-ji. What a pleasant surprise!'

'A very good morning to you, Ramya-ji. Thought I would spy on both of you and listen to your girlie talk.'

'Spy? No, three is company!' quipped Ramya.

For some time, they walked in silence. Vibha stopped for a minute to say, 'If this was Delhi, we would have found a humble *chai* shop somewhere that'll give us hot tea.'

'May be with a crisp *mathri* to go with the *chai*,' said Sandeep, warming up to the idea. 'Anyway, let's sit for a while and imagine we're having *chai*,' said Sandeep.

They found a shaded place with four garden seats arranged in a square.

'Missed you yesterday,' said Vibha. 'Hope you had a restful sleep. Cooking for 10 people, plus the family!'

'And that wasn't all. There were some painful discoveries too,' said Ramya.

Sandeep and Vibha kept quiet. The birds chirped in the background. It felt so good to be out and away from the relentless chores that awaited the retired women professionals in the US.

Ramya was silent as her thoughts went back to another dinner for which she was invited as a guest. It was hosted by Alka's daughter. Renu was also there. Both of them were the typical mothers who came every year to visit their children's house in the US.

The dinner had unfolded like a scene that seemed like a flashback to the 1960s or '70s in India.

The men sat in a more spacious area of the living room, engrossed in conversation about their work, their new cars, the mortgage for a new house, their next vacation and the soccer or other sports played by their children.

Rajiv took his mother to this group.

'Hello everyone. Meet my Mom. I insisted that she come here for a break after Dad passed on. Actually, she is waiting to fix up a consultancy with some good clinics there. With her long track record in working with Apollo Hospitals, that shouldn't be difficult at all.'

'No, not at all,' chorused many of them.

'You're sure to get some good offers, Madam. The one important thing is, you need to be careful about the clinic you choose,' said Mishra-ji, one of the fathers.

'Oh yes,' said Ramya, settling on the seat next to him. 'Still, I can do with some advice,' she smiled.

'Sure Madam,' he said, genially. 'Actually, what I meant is, one needs to do thorough homework about the background of a set-up and the one who heads it. For instance, after I retired from my government job as a Chief Financial Advisor, some good friends advised me to avoid companies that offered to hire me with fancy designations and salaries. They asked me to opt for a PSU instead.'

'What's a PSU, Uncle?' asked a friend of Rajiv.

'Public Sector Undertaking. And I'll tell you why. If there is some litigation or dispute, I don't get directly involved, especially if I insist on prefixing my appointment with an 'Honorary' before Advisor. It's the responsibility of the man who heads the unit.'

'Thank God,' said Ramya.

'Yes, Madam. At this age, who wants to get into disputes for which you're not responsible? I don't want a big salary or a fancy designation. My needs are few. I just want a peaceful life,' said Mishra-ji.

'Aunty, Dad lives alone now, with a housekeeper,' his son, Sanjay, explained. 'We too don't want any complications in his life. My Mom passed on two years back.'

'Oh, I'm so sorry to hear,' said Ramya. 'Yes, Sanjay. What's more important is a safe and peaceful life for your father.'

'Yes Auntie, absolutely.'

'Initially, I had other plans for Mom,' said Rajiv. 'I wanted her to apply for a green card right away so that she can stay with us for a longer time. But now, Mom is keen on working.'

'Show your Mom around, Rajiv. Give her a good vacation,' said a friend.

'Sure, I will.'

***

Ramya laughed to herself as she thought of the so-called green card and her talk with Vibha about the colour green, the 'sick' colour that had changed their children into unrecognizably selfish people. The green card continues to be referred to colloquially as 'green', despite it being printed in pink now! She knew some 'GC holders' in Delhi. They would shut their house up for six months, pay a retainer salary to their drivers and house help, lock up their cars in the garage and leave for the US. Few months later, they would return to a dusty, termite-ridden home, get rid of things that were covered with fungus, clean up their house, often by themselves because the drivers and help would have bolted with their money to work for new employers. The car would need an elaborate servicing to make it roadworthy again. What a restless life! To our unspoken question if they enjoyed those six months of being away from the grind, we would get an unstated answer that expressed resentment against their children. It was an answer we felt on the skin, wordlessly.

The men had resumed their conversation, filling each other's glasses. Ramya noticed that she was the lone woman there. She got up with an 'Excuse me' and moved over to join the women who sat huddled around the dining table. Some of them had pulled a few lounge chairs for themselves. A few women expressed their condolences to Ramya and inquired about how she was managing alone.

'Life must be very tough without your husband,' said one.

'It is. But I'm looking forward to working in some good clinics,' said Ramya.

'You're lucky that you're a doctor. With your experience in Apollo Hospitals, you'll easily get work,' said another.

'Let's hope so. I met Mishra-ji just now, Sanjay's father. I felt sorry to hear that he too lost his wife, about two years back.'

'Yes. He now works with an organisation, but feels lonely. So, he comes to Sanjay's place every year,' said a lady.

'He comes every year? Does he do the cooking while he is here?' asked Ramya. The question was out before she could hold it back.

For a moment, the lady stared back at her, very puzzled by the query. The silence that followed was broken by a young woman who said, 'Why, Auntie? I do the cooking,' she said, her hands pressed together. 'Namaste. I'm Rashmi, Sanjay's wife,' she added, with a pleasant smile.

Lucky Mishra-ji, thought Ramya. So, a widower in the US gets a better deal.

A few women got into a long discussion about the methods of making Hyderabadi vegetable *biryani* and *bagara baingan* with eggplant. Two women got up and went to the kitchen to help Alka. One of them fried *puri*s, while the other, Ratna, fried *paneer* and *palak pakoda*s for starters and drained them in a large perforated steel bowl.

'Hey, Ratna! Keep some *pakoda*s and *chutney* for us separately in a vessel,' Alka cautioned her. 'If you take the entire thing to the living room, the men will finish it in no time, and there'll be nothing left for us.' The women nodded and giggled.

'Okay,' said Ratna, putting away some of the *pakoda*s in a steel vessel. She kept the rest in a glass bowl, arranged it on a tray with smaller bowls for green *chutney* and tomato ketchup and took it to the other end of the room.

***

Dinner over, Rajiv turned back from his driver's seat to ask Ramya, 'Enjoyed yourself, Amma?'

'There was a lot of talk about *biryani* and *bagara baingan*. Will go home and note the details in my diary, lest I forget,' she replied, thankful that they couldn't see her wry smile within the darkness of the car.

'Who talked about them, Amma?' asked Chitra. 'Actually, these aunties make excellent dishes whenever they visit here. So, the minute any friend announces about his or her mother coming over, our entire circle is happy.'

Chitra chirped on. 'Amma, did Alka Aunty ask you about making batter for *idli-dosa*? Ever since we told her you were due to come, she was so eager to learn from you. I have an idea. Why don't you give a demo in her house, kind of teach her how you soak rice and *urad dal* in her house? Then she'll be very clear about how exactly we do it. The same day you can also explain how to make coconut *chutney* and *sambar* to her. Aunty loves it.'

'Not just Aunty, the entire family and our circle of North Indian friends love *idli-dosa* with *chutney* and *sambar*,' chipped in Rajiv. Ramya felt thankful again that they couldn't see her grim face in the darkness of the back seat. 'Both Alka Aunty and Renu Aunty are such sweethearts,' continued Chitra. 'They cook extra and often pack takeaways for us. I don't have to cook anything the next day.'

***

Ramya's thoughts came back to the day before when she had cooked dinner for 10 guests. It had depleted her of all energy. She remembered how it had ended.

'I'm very tired, Rajiv. I don't think I've any strength left to clear up the table now,' said Ramya.

'Oh, Amma gets tired so easily,' said Chitra, lips curling.

'Well, I guess I'm not used to so much cooking. When I come home, there's Savitri to cook for me. But I suppose when I come here, I've to merge with the rest of the visiting women, the various aunties,' said Ramya.

Rajiv stood beside Chitra with a sheepish smile. He avoided her eyes. Where's the Rajiv who would pitch in to help for big things and small, seeing his father navigating his wheelchair from room to room. '*Amma, you're getting late for Apollo. Leave the rest of the work to me. I'll manage.*'

'Come to think of it, Rajiv, it's a big party scene here. So long as the aunties keep visiting, they'll keep it going, I guess,' said Ramya and went to her room. She shut the door, firmly bolted it from inside and sat on a lounge chair to collect herself.

Ramya and Seshadri had given Rajiv everything they could. He was for them, both a son and a daughter rolled into one. Why should I think of all that with an ache, she argued with herself? The mirror of the dressing table, placed at some distance from the chair, reflected her ruminative image. 'I'm disappointed with you,' she whispered to her image. 'After all that you learnt in the *Gita* class about *karma*, of working without thinking of the fruits of your labour, after reading that "when you act in such knowledge, you can free yourself from the bondage of work", why do you still get angry with Rajiv? Should he matter?'

That particular class studying Chapter 10, verse 10 of *Bhagavad Gita* had the most vociferous Q&A session. They felt encouraged by the London-based British speaker who had a robust sense of humour. Laughing heartily at their questions, he called them a spirited bunch of disciples who'll surely fight their way through life. Most of the people in the class admitted that *karma-yoga* and *buddhi-yoga* could be understood intellectually, but were actually very difficult to practice. 'Be in direct communion with Sri Krishna', declared the speaker in the end. 'You'll find that it's a goal worth pursuing because it'll liberate you from expecting certain results to happen.' Ramya realised that navigating the teachings of the *Gita* is a quest in itself.

Did it matter so much whenever such thankless moments cropped up during my work with Apollo, she wondered. Like the parents of this girl who had a severe neurological disorder. How they shouted at me one day that I was unable to 'cure her', despite their spending so much money for her treatment.

'Well, I've done my best, the rest is…' Ramya had argued.

'Is this your best?' hissed the mother. Two ward boys and her junior doctor had come in, hearing the commotion. They ushered the angry couple out of her room, but it left her seething with rage. She battled with the wish to toss her white coat and drive off that very minute. To think that she had even prayed for the girl. It became just another case for Apollo's Grievance Cell for Doctors that protested against the rough deal they got from some families. They went on strike, twice.

Slowly, her mind got stilled. Someone or something was asking her to be more accepting. That had its own comfort. Be happy, she told herself. No, be proud that you could do a lot for that girl, for your husband Seshadri, for your son Rajiv and others. Ramya opened her eyes to realise that she had dozed off on the chair. It was 2 am. She got up, changed into her night wear and went to bed.

The following morning, she brushed, washed her face, tidied up her hair and went out of her room. The house hadn't woken up yet. On the way to the kitchen, she was startled by a sight: the used plates, glasses, cutlery and other things from dinner lay scattered on the table, just the way they were last night. She went to the kitchen, made coffee for herself and took it to her room.

***

The birds chirped in the background as the three of them sat quietly on the garden seats. Ramya turned to Vibha and said, 'Rajiv's 10 dinner guests included some parents of their friends. One woman had difficulty speaking in English. She asked me in Hindi how to make *idli* batter. Another asked me the difference between *dosa* and *uthappam*, while a third inquired how I make lemon rice. Their talk was all about food.'

Sandeep chuckled.

'And that's not all. After the guests left, I felt utterly exhausted. So, I told Rajiv and Chitra that I don't have any strength left in me to clear up and clean the dining table. I went to my room and bolted the door. Guess what I saw next morning?'

'What?' asked Vibha.

'The dining table was just the way as I had left it. Neither one of them had cleared it up.'

'Oh God! This is too bad,' said Sandeep.

'Yes, and no.'

'What do you mean, Ramya?' asked Vibha.

'It means I needed a catalytic agent, and I got it! See… as long as I keep coming here, in their perception I'll continue to be one of the aunties who'll cook endlessly. To be very honest, it's not fair to the aunties either, all the Alkas and Renus. They're not getting any younger. They're our contemporaries.

Anyway, it's entirely their call if they still choose to come here. As for me, I don't have to visit Rajiv.'

Vibha and Sandeep watched her silently.

'So, in a way, I'm thankful for this shock,' said Ramya. 'Otherwise, I may have got into a mind-numbing routine of travelling to the US to visit Rajiv. After Rajiv and Chitra left for office, I called my travel agent and got a booking done for the earliest flight back to Delhi,' said Ramya.

'Oh! Splendid idea! Please ask your agent if he could book us too, if possible, on the same flight,' said Vibha.

'What! But why?'

'Yes, Ramya. Actually, Sandeep and I also had a serious talk about this. We want to return the soonest!'

Ramya laughed as she got up. She dusted the back of her track pants, straightened her T-shirt, and smiled at Vibha and Sandeep.

'I guess our *Gita* class beckons!' she said.

'Yes!' said Sandeep, with a wide grin. Vibha's eyes absorbed once more the trees dripping with changing colours, before she joined them on their walk towards home.

LADIES' WATCH

By the time she walked around the Ortega Park for the second time, the gentle drizzle had become a purposeful rain. Savitri covered Malaika's head with the end of her saree and hurried into the first shelter near the water fountain. The place was already crowded with the compulsive morning-walkers of Sunnyvale. She recognized some of the regulars. Four people stood at the fringe of the crowd, waiting for the first clear moment to step out. Savitri recalled how just 10 minutes back these four were performing t'ai chi gracefully, led by their nimble Chinese instructor in an open section of the park.

Savitri wiped Malaika's face and shook her head as the child begged her to let her walk in the rain. She removed her wristwatch, wiped it carefully and put it away in the small pouch that hung on her shoulder. It certainly couldn't be a watch that was waterproof. At $5.00 USD, it was perhaps the most inexpensive watch on sale—dirt-cheap as they called it.

Far more expensive watches at home had stopped working because of water seepage. A good amount was spent in repairing them. But her watch could never be repaired, her son Vijay Bhaskar had said. In case it stops working, it just has to be thrown away, and one buys a new one. It was a disposable watch.

'Here, Mom,' Vijay had said, giving her the watch. 'I bought this watch for you. Can't guarantee for how long it'll work though. It may keep going for the next four or six months or it could stop after a week from now. You never know. Depends on your luck.' he laughed. 'Ah, I did check if it's a ladies' watch, so you can use it,' he smiled.

That was a good one year back but the watch had showed no signs of stopping. Ever. It had gone on ticking resolutely much to the surprise of Vijay Bhaskar and his wife Asha. They had grown tired of marveling and joking about its tenacity, consigning the matter to the background as one of those things that goes on its own steam and can't be explained.

'Come, my pet,' said Savitri to Malaika. 'It has stopped raining. Let's hurry or we'll get late.'

There were lots of others who walked along as they came out of Ortega Park. Americans, Chinese, Indians from different cultures—Gujaratis Punjabis, South Indians, a few Bengalis. Savitri and Malaika crossed the school ground. Home was just two streets away. She held Malaika by the hand and crossed the street. It started drizzling again. Why did I forget the umbrella, she thought. Because it was so bright in the morning with the sky a clear, innocent blue. That's California for you in November. Unpredictable.

On reaching home, Savitri took out the watch from her pouch and placed it in the right end corner of the kitchen counter, in the usual place reserved for it. She gave Malaika a bath, dressed her, opened the shelves in the kitchen and asked her. 'What cereal do you want today? Wheat Checks, Cheerios, Lucky Charms...?'

'Cheerios!' said Malaika. She settled her at the dining table, poured milk into her bowl of cereal and said, 'Come on, hurry. You must get ready. Mummy and Daddy are taking you out in a while.' Malaika scooped up her cereal and smiled at her grandmother.

'Want some fresh strawberries with the cereal, precious?' asked Savitri. The child nodded happily. Savitri cut the strawberries into small pieces and put them in her bowl. She stood for a moment enjoying the sight of luscious strawberries vanishing into her small mouth. Then she returned to preparing a picnic lunch for the family. Briskly, the *puri*s were being fried in hot oil when Asha, her daughter-in-law came in, floating in the aroma of her shampoo, her skin glowing with health.

'Will lunch be ready, Mummy, for us to take along?' she asked.

'Of course. Come and have breakfast, both of you. Where's Vijay?'

'Having a shower. Anything I can do to help, Mummy?' asked Asha, standing at the doorway.

'Nothing really. You get ready.'

'All right. I'll go dry my hair. Are you sure you don't want to come with us?'

'Actually, I have tons of things to do. I'll come with you another day,' said Savitri, garnishing the potato-onion *masala* to go with the *puris*. Lemon rice was ready. She packed the *puris* and potato-onion *masala* in separate casseroles, packed the rest of the stuff, kept bottles of water, juices, Goldfish, Graham Crackers and Nilla cookies for Malaika, fruits and then napkins, paper plates, spoons and so on into the boot of the car. She hurried in from the garage and glanced at her watch. It's 10:00 already!

'Vijay, Asha', she called and laid out their breakfast. She served them *uppuma* with coconut-coriander *chutney*.

'It's yummy!' said Vijay, taking large helpings of the *uppuma*.

Savitri collected a few of Malaika's toys for the rear seat. Giving Malaika her favourite velvety monkey and panda bear in hand, she strapped her in her seat.

'Why don't you come along, Mummy?' asked Vijay as he eased himself into the driver's seat. Savitri smiled and waved them goodbye. With one touch of the remote, the garage door came rolling down and she was plunged in darkness.

She switched on the light. It flooded the huge pile of laundry in a large rattan basket and showed the huge utensils on the left, holding soaked rice and black gram, waiting to be ground for *idli* on the motorised stone-grinder. With other things strewn around or stashed away, the garage looked comfortably shabby, like the 'common-room' back home in her father's house in Thumkur. Three daughters and their mother shared it. Savitri hurried into the washroom, had a shower, came out, dressed and lit the lamp in the shrine for her morning prayers. She made herself a cup of coffee to go with her breakfast. Sunnyvale had decided to be sunny again. Bright light poured in through the window and the sky wore its clear, innocent blue as if nothing had happened. Mustn't waste this bit of sunlight, let me do the laundry quickly, she said to herself, gulping down her coffee.

Back in the garage, the clothes swished in soap water, the machine droned on as she sat waiting, sitting on a low stool near the machine that was grinding rice for *idli* batter.

Thak! *Thak*! *Thak*!

Sounds of damp clothes flung on a sloping, rough, stone-topped platform in the backyard with a bucket and tap on a side. That was how they washed clothes way back, in Thumkur. *Thak*! *Thak*! The clothes got a thrashing on the pitted stone platform. Then they were hand-rinsed in water, squeezed and put out to dry. Savitri, her elder sister Mangalam and her younger sister Radha took turns washing the clothes of the entire household, taking particular care to brush and clean their brother Madhav's shirt, shorts and undergarments. These had to be dried in the sunniest part of the washing line.

Savitri's elder sister Mangalam was the first child of the family. 'Mangalam' meant the completion of an event. She was named Mangalam perhaps in the anxious hope that it would be the end of girl-children for the family. But Savitri followed Mangalam, and then there was Radha. Madhav came last after three girls, ushering in much celebration and exchange of sweets. By now all the three girls realised that they were born experimentally, as a means toward that eternal quest for a son. Girls number one, two, three were just passages to make way for that one boy, Madhav.

He didn't have to wash clothes. The girls washed his clothes, they assisted in cooking, cleaning the house, ran errands for the family, sewed clothes and the household ran like a well-greased machine. Mangalam and Savitri were good in studies, but they were pulled out of school so that the money could be saved for Madhav who was enrolled in an expensive school. Year after year, he failed to qualify in his exams. Hesitantly, Mangalam asked if she may resume her studies now. She was sternly told to take responsibility for the housework, as befits an eldest daughter, and look after Madhav. She took him to school and brought him back every single day. As for Radha, she never saw the face of a school but spent time languishing at home, reading her sisters' old school books.

'Madhav needs extra nourishment. His health isn't too robust, which is why he is unable to study,' said the parents, plying him with thickened milk, butter, lentils, vegetables, creamy yoghurt and fruits. The buttermilk for the three girls got further diluted with water. They did not get any vegetables and for them, fruits were only for looking. Yet Madhav continued to fall ill frequently. At the first whimper he would be rushed to the doctor, medicines would be procured, and more water added to the buttermilk for the girls.

The doctor's advice for physical activities, sports, exercise and diet control to combat his increasing obesity went unheeded. They changed his doctor instead and resumed giving him thickened milk, creamy yoghurt, butter, rich *kheer* and sweets as before. New clothes were made for him as he was fast outgrowing his shirts and shorts.

Mangalam and Savitri registered themselves for their studies through a correspondence course as it was inexpensive. Mangalam did exceedingly well and studied hard well into the night. A week before her exams, she came down with a raging fever.

'Don't give her anything to eat,' declared her father. 'You must always starve a fever. Just put a damp cloth over her forehead and the fever will come down. She'll be all right in a few days.'

Her mother made her a thin rice gruel. The fever couldn't stand much starvation. It left Mangalam within two days.

'See?' the father exulted. 'I told you that a doctor is quite unnecessary for such fevers. Good. Mangalam, now you can go to the ration shop for this month's supply. Radha, go with your sister and help her carry the stuff,' he commanded. Savitri had her exams the following day. She stayed at home and studied whenever she found the time from helping her mother make snacks for the evening.

***

Images swirled in her consciousness. There was her marriage that left no imprint in her memory. Her husband was a few years older than her. He died soon after Vijay Bhaskar was born. Savitri spent an entire lifetime bringing up Vijay and educating him. It was rewarding, for he had done very well for himself and effortlessly got a good job in the US.

Suddenly, Savitri became aware that all the noises were coming only from her head, and that the garage had indeed fallen silent. It was so quiet in there. The washing machine had also stopped. The laundry was done. She glanced quickly at the steel utensils with the grains waiting to be ground for *idli*. She put the soaked rice, switched on the stone grinder, then took the pile of clothes in two buckets to the backyard and put them out to dry. On the way back to the kitchen, she noticed that there was another pile of clothes, clean and dry, on the sofa in the living room. She rushed to the kitchen, checked the *kabuli chana* that had been soaked overnight, put them into the pressure cooker and set it on the gas burner. Asha loves *chana*. Must make them all a nice dinner after they return from their picnic trip, she thought.

Oh dear, she glanced at the watch on the counter. It was 10:45. But it felt like she had spent 20 years recalling her childhood in Thumkur inside the garage. Must rush with the *idli*-grinding, she said to herself and went to the garage. The rice was done. She put the soaked black gram and switched on the stone grinder again. It swung into action rhythmically as Savitri stepped into the kitchen and briskly prepared the garnishing for *kabuli chana*. She also made Vijay's favourite *sambar* with green bell peppers and potatoes. The pressure cooker whistled furiously. Savitri looked at her watch. I'll let it cook on low fire for another 10 minutes till the *chana* is done soft and tender, she thought, reducing the flame.

Back in the garage, she scooped up the black gram paste over the rice paste, sprinkled salt and mixed them evenly with a long wooden ladle till her arm ached. Fatigue engulfed her body. She sat in the stillness for a minute, doing nothing.

***

Dinner items done, she sat down to a simple lunch. She had no appetite whatsoever. The yoghurt was so unnaturally thick. She mixed it with water till it looked like the buttermilk of Thumkur, and washed down her rice with it. She put some of the newly made *sambar* and *kabuli chana* on her plate to taste. They were fine enough. The dough for *roti*s was also ready. O God, she had forgotten that pile of dried clothes on the sofa in the living room. She folded them up neatly and took them to her room. They were a mix of clothes. She separated them into Vijay's, Asha's, Malaika's and hers and placed them tidily in two rows on one side of her bed. Let them be here for the time being, she thought. I'll take them over to Vijay's room later.

Must keep some orange juice ready for Malaika. They'll be back any moment. She ensured that the carton of Minute Maid was there, and put out Malaika's favourite doggie-face mug before she looked at her watch. It was 2:30 now. There's time for a small nap, I feel so tired, she thought.

Savitri went to her room and stretched herself on the free side of her bed, along the row of neatly folded clothes on the other side of the bed. She removed her wristwatch and placed it beside the row of folded clothes. It felt blissful to close her eyes. After Malaika rests, I'll ask her about the day's trip. Then read her a story and see everything through her lustrous eyes. Tomorrow, I'll take her to Ortega Park, make her sit on the swing or watch her come down the slide with a shriek of delight, her dress billowing in the wind, her sleeves flapping like a butterfly. Malaika, the new-age girl growing up in California. A lovely butterfly with the sun on her wings.

***

Savitri was the caterpillar that shuffled about awkwardly toward the ration shop in Thumkur, forever hungry, looking for green leaves and fruits to chew. It searched on its three pairs of true legs and wobbled along. The prolegs in the middle made it slow in movement. There were no leaves in sight, still it kept moving, not sure if it can starve its way to staying alive till the next week. But it stayed alive somehow. One day it shook itself free of the integument, raised its head confidently and became Asha in Sunnyvale, a hard-working professional who brings home plenty of green leaves and fruits. And then there is the beautiful butterfly Malaika, catching the sun on her billowing skirt as she went forward and backward on the swing. Malaika smiled at her grandmother. For Savitri, it felt like drinking clear, sparkling spring water. She ran her fingers through the soft, young hair of her grandchild. The bed felt soft and downy too, after the day's work.

***

They called a doctor known to a close friend, or else who would home-visit anyone in the US? He made for the bed straight away and took in the sleeping figure of Savitri. He pushed away the neat stack of washed clothes kept in two rows beside the sleeping Savitri.

'For God's sake, allow her to breathe. What's this pile of clothes doing on her bed? Take them away,' he ordered with impatience. Asha moved in, looking embarrassed. She took one pile of clothes in her hands.

'Mummy must've...' she began to explain, her voice agitated.

'No, no! She needs to breathe freely...Take them away,' the doctor cut in, stethoscope around his ears. He placed the end piece on Savitri's chest while he felt her pulse at the same time. He straightened up, looked in silence at the calm figure on the bed and folded his hands in front. He shook his head, and then turned to Vijay.

'I'm sorry Vijay. I'm really very sorry. Your Mom...'

'But Doctor, she was fine when we left her,' protested Vijay, his throat going dry. Asha moved in to collect the next pile of clothes. The doctor pushed it towards her, and then saw the faded brown wristwatch beside Savitri.

'What's this old watch doing here? It has stopped at three. It's nearing six now!' he said, giving it to Vijay.

'Three? Then that must be the time when my mother died,' said Vijay, his eyes welling up.

'What! How can you say for sure?' retorted the doctor. Strange, how incomprehensible, his eyes said.

'Because Doctor, this watch stopped working at last. At long last,' replied Vijay, burying his face in his hands.

'Vijay Bhaskar, what are you saying? Have a grip over yourself. I know this is hard on you. It's very shocking indeed to come home and see your mother gone. I'm really very sorry,' he said, placing an arm over Vijay's shoulder. It shook, racked by his sobs.

ANNAPURNA BHAVAN

The next two hours were free for Tara to spend them any way she wished to. She wanted to maximize the time she spent with her dear friend Sunita who was recovering from a surgery in a hospital near Mylapore, Chennai. She sat with her in her private room, took her lunch tray from the hospital staff, and personally served her as she reclined on the bed. 'I must somehow restore Sunita to Sunita', she told herself. 'She was such a chirpy, positive person. How did this surgery take away all that from her?' In between sips of soups, mashed rice with *dal* and vegetables, Tara gently coaxed Sunita to eat well, to get strong so that her discharge papers could be processed and she could return to the comfort of her home and slowly resume her work online. 'It's the digital era', she said, as if it needed a reminder. 'We now have the wonderful opportunity to work from home until one can resume working in-office. So Sunita, work towards that goal. We're all waiting to see you on your feet again,' she encouraged. Sunita gave her a weak smile.

'What about your lunch, Tara? It's well past lunch time,' she asked.

'No worries. I have a car at my disposal, I've made arrangements for my lunch. I'll have a quick bite somewhere and join my family,' she assured.

'Come on, have some custard. You must eat well, Sunita. Promise?'

Sunita nodded, her eyes incongruously bright on her wan face.

Tara tucked her back into bed, said goodbye with a thumbs-up sign and came out of the room.

***

Waiting for the elevator, Tara recalled how she had warded off all the lunch-suggestions by her family before she came to the hospital.

She told her family that she would visit Sunita in the hospital, then grab a quick lunch somewhere and then join them for the rest of the day. Instantly, her family had pulled out their phones and googled restaurants that would qualify as 'good' even if it meant driving some distance. Tara said New Woodlands Hotel is bang on at Radhakrishnan Salai in Mylapore, so she could use the time to be with her friend, then have a quick meal and join them. A chorus of voices said New Woodlands was just 'okay'. 'It has improved a bit, has a Family Section where you can get some privacy', still it wasn't one of the best, they argued rather patronizingly. They suggested other outlets. One of them advised that she drive past New Woodlands, get on to Anna Salai road and reach the Taj Connemara. 'It has The Verandah restaurant with a multi-cuisine buffet. You can mix and match the dishes any which way you like and eat your fill.'

'Or try Raintree Hotel,' said another. 'It's also on Anna Salai road.'

'Isn't there a Raintree at Alwarpet? I heard it has a nice restaurant on the terrace, appropriately called Above Sea Level', said another.

They showed her the directions on Google Maps, and advised her to follow them on her phone.

Poor New Woodlands, she thought, now relegated to a middle class eating joint, used only as a landmark by her family. '*Go past New Woodlands...*' Ruthlessly bypassed after all these new fancy upscale restaurants that have mushroomed in the city.

'Fine, thanks a lot. I'll go to one of these and join you all soon. Don't worry, I'm on my own turf. I'll sail through my way speaking in Tamil. The driver, Dorai, seems like a nice chap. Bye for now,' she waved and was off to the parking space. Inside the car, Tara wondered why nobody in her family thought of

Dorai and where he would have his lunch. Why ask him to eat somewhere and then go to The Verandah, or Above Sea Level to pick her up? That will delay things unnecessarily. Why not have lunch at New Woodlands, both Dorai and I, she thought. That would be neat. It will cut down the waiting time. She had rushed to the hospital and was soon ushered into Sunita's private room. She was glad she got some time to linger with her and coax her to eat lunch.

***

Tara came out of the hospital and got into her car.

'Dorai, please take me to New Woodlands,' she said. 'We'll both have lunch there, and then we'll drive up to where my family is waiting for me,' she said.

He turned back and smiled. 'Amma, I'll drop you at New Woodlands and go to another place for my lunch.'

'Oh no! That will take time. That's exactly why I suggested New Woodlands so that both of us can eat there and then move on.'

'No worries, Amma. My *votel* is also nearby only. It won't take long.'

'I see. Why Dorai, don't you like the food in New Woodlands? I've been there. It was so good'.

'Not just good Amma, it's excellent,' he nodded.

'Then why do you want to go somewhere else?'

Dorai turned away and stared through the windscreen.

'What's the matter, Dorai? Please tell me. Of course, you can eat wherever you prefer to.'

He turned back again, this time with a shy smile on his face.

'Amma, how can I explain? You won't understand.'

'What!'

'Yes Amma, if I mention some dishes that only small, humble votels offer, you may not even know those items.'

'Such as?'

He grinned, but lowered his eyes. 'Amma, there's a small place called Annapurna Bhavan. It serves rare things like *paruppu podi, mormilagai, vatral kuzhambu, karuvadaam, palapp pazham*, a tumbler with *neer mor* garnished with *karuveppilai* and ginger and much more…'

Tara burst out laughing when she noticed that Dorai was almost salivating when he listed his favourite dishes.

'Wonderful, Dorai! I know those dishes very well because I've grown up on them. I'm also very fond of them as they remind me of my mother's cooking when I was small. I'm glad you've located a place that has all these.'

'Amma, not only do they make these dishes well, they don't just put it all out in cups on a large plate. They serve, Amma, item by item, and they serve so ungrudgingly. It is as if *satshat* Devi Annapurni has descended, to give us food like a mother.'

'Maybe that's why it's called Annapurna Bhavan!' said Tara, laughing.

'Hee hee, yes!' chuckled Dorai, nodding his head vigorously.

'Fine. Let's both eat there.'

'Oh no! It's not a place for you, Amma. I just can't take you there. *Saar* will be angry with me if he comes to know,' he protested.

'Then we don't tell *Saar*, simple!' she smiled. 'Dorai, I just told you how much I love the items you mentioned. It has been a very long time since I ate those things. I live in far-off Delhi, you see.'

'I know, I know, but Amma, it's not a suitable place for you. Saar phoned me about The Verandah and the other place, Sea something...'

'Above Sea Level. No! I don't want to go to all those places. Just take me to Annapurna Bhavan. I'll tell Saar I went to The Verandah,' said Tara, firmly.

'Oh Amma, how can you tell a lie like that? Please listen to me. It has no parking area. I've to park the car on the main road and then walk through two narrow lanes to reach the *votel*. It's a small one, you see.'

'I can very well walk on a lane. Come on, Dorai. Start the car or we'll be late.'

***

Tara got out of the car and Dorai led the way to another street that was cutting the main road at an angle. Vendors in carts selling vegetables and fruits were lined on both sides of the street. They walked for about 200 metres when Dorai said 'This way, Amma', pointing to the right. Tara followed him on a narrow lane that had a mix of houses, grocery shops and places for repairing cycle and scooter. A few stray cows ambled about lazily. Annapurna Bhavan was on the opposite side, joining two small buildings. Even as they entered the restaurant, the smell of food wafted over to the small reception in the front.

'Do you have a family section?' inquired Dorai.

'Ah, Yes. But I'm sorry. It's full. If you wait for about half an hour, I can find a table in the Family Section for Madam.'

'It doesn't matter,' said Tara. 'I'll go to the general section.'

'No, no! Can't you try, please?' pleaded Dorai.

The man at the reception thought for a minute, but shook his head to indicate that it was 'full'.

'What I could do is to find Madam a table in the Ladies' section, will that do?' he asked.

'Okay, okay, at least do that. Thank you,' said Dorai, still disgruntled by the whole idea—a bad one, according to him.

He came with her till the door of the Ladies' section and then pointed to the left.

'I'll be going there, Amma, to the general section,' he said.

'Have a good lunch Dorai. No need to hurry. We have enough time,' smiled Tara, going into the hall that had multiple rows of tables. They were already occupied by women who were blithely chatting with one another. The hall echoed with their loud laughter and uninhibited chatter. Just as Dorai said, there were no large plates with multiple cups. Food was being served course by course on a banana leaf, like in a wedding. She was ushered to a table.

'One meal, Amma?' asked a waiter.

'Yes please'.

He placed a large banana leaf on the table, served her a steel tumbler of water and waited. She looked at him for a moment, then took the cue from others and sprinkled water on the leaf. She then cleaned it with her hand, like the women were doing. He placed another tumbler and poured thin buttermilk into it from a steel jug. It was flavoured with curry leaves, ginger and salt.

'I will tell the boys to serve you a meal, Amma,' he said and left.

Tara sipped at the buttermilk and looked around. Already, some of the women seemed to be half way into their meal. The hall swarmed with women in brightly coloured sarees, their glass and gold bangles clinking on their wrists, their faces eager to catch up on news while they went on a sustained friendly banter over their lunch. It looked like many of them were friends who had fixed up a date and time to meet here for a girls' day out, thought Tara. She was amazed to see the way they could keep a lively thread of conversation going while at the same time, they were mindful of what reached their 'leaf' and what got missed. Tara was amused to note that each one of them referred to her leaf impersonally as 'this leaf', instead of 'my leaf'. Some women called out to the waiters variously as '*Anne*', '*Empaa*' and so on and said, 'Here, give more *poriyal* to this leaf. And that leaf needs rice, more rice! She called out for you, but you didn't hear. *Aiye* Shenbagam, you asked for rice, *di*!' said the woman looking after her friend's 'leaf' along with her own. Tara noticed how they kept a tab on each other, like they were members of a family.

They had no qualms whatsoever, in demanding the men to serve them more. On the table next to her on left, and on the one opposite, *sambar*, and then *rasam* was being served. Another boy ladled out spoons of something. Instantly, the women mixed the rice and brought their hand to their nose to smell. Tara turned her face to the left and saw the same thing. Women brought their hands up instantly to their nose to smell.

Her meal came with varieties of vegetables, *poriyal*, *karuvadam*, fried *appalam*, and other things from the four-chambered cornucopia that the server carried so deftly. He put some *paruppu podi* in a corner of her leaf and asked her to make a hole in the center. Then he poured some *til* oil into it. Tara motioned him to come closer to hear her.

'*Empaa*, why are those women smelling the oil the minute it is poured into their rice?'

'Because it is not oil, Amma. It is pure *nei* that is poured for *sambar*, *rasam* and rice. I'll also be serving *nei* as soon as the boy gets hot rice for you.' He smiled.

'Oh. All right. But why do they smell it, each one of them?'

The man laughed till his shoulders shook. 'Amma, you seem to be new here. These women are all so clever and shrewd, you see. They want to check instantly if we're serving them pure *nei*, or craftily passing off some oil as *nei*', he grinned. 'They'll catch us by the neck if we cheat! Nobody can fool them. They're all well trained in cooking, you see. They just come here for a change, to enjoy one day when they don't have to serve their family or eat with their family watching. Okay, now let me ask the boy to hurry up with your rice,' he said, walking away with an amused smile.

Tara was fascinated. The women were clever to the core, and didn't want to take any chance. *Ghee* had better be genuine *ghee*, or else…!

Rice was served steaming hot. She mixed it with *paruppu podi* and *til* oil, and relished the taste. It transported her to the days when her mother gave her and her siblings *paruppu podi* whenever she couldn't find the time to make *sambar* and was busy with other things. *Paruppu podi* had gone out of the menu, and the lexicon of Tamil cuisine. A simple dish of fresh sautéed string beans with soft grated coconut, potato *poriyal* and the *koottu* made with white pumpkin—everything was tasty. More rice was served with hot *sambar* into which the man poured *ghee*. Tara could smell it without bringing the mix to her nose. The man gave her a broad smile. Tara noticed that it was the same man who had served her *til* oil with *paruppu podi* and explained why women instantly took their hands to their nose the minute *ghee* was served.

'Don't want to smell the *nei*, Amma?' he smiled, with a mischievous twinkle in his eyes. Tara smiled back at him, nodded and smelt her hand just the way the women were doing. The aroma of pure *ghee* filled her heart. The man laughed and said, 'I'll now bring *rasam*, Amma. Want some more rice?' he asked.

'No, I've enough rice. Just bring me *rasam*.'

'Very well, Amma. You've hardly eaten anything,' he said, before he went.

'This leaf didn't get *payasam*,' said a woman loudly, on the next table.

'This leaf needs some *koottu*.'

'This leaf...'

'This leaf...'

'Anne, this leaf...have you forgotten?'

'No, no! How can that be? I'll get it for you in a minute.'

Tara watched, fascinated by the informal camaraderie between the women and the men who served them. The woman sitting at the opposite table told her waiter, 'Anne, why are you ignoring this leaf? You've forgotten to even ask me if I need more rice or *poriyal*.'

'Ayyo, excuse me *thangacchi*, I didn't do it on purpose. Someone else was calling me and...here you go,' he said, ladling out rice with a large curved serving spoon. 'What would you like with it, *morkuzhambu* or *sambar* again?'

'Both!' said the woman, bursting into peals of laughter that was echoed by her companions at the table. One woman teased her for stuffing herself with enormous quantity of *sambar* rice. 'Watch out Shenbagam, or you'll put on weight,' she warned.

'Shut up, di! I feel like I've come to my mother's house. I can eat as much as I want without...'

'Without your husband's elder sister, or his widowed aunt, or your mother-in-law staring at you with a frown?' she helpfully completed the sentence for her.

'Exactly! They think we women should not eat heartily, it's considered unseemly,' she said, slurping her *rasam*.

'Well then, let them come and take a look at us. We'll show them how decorous we are while eating,' the woman laughed. Other women from the tables joined her and there were squeals of laughter all around that group.

'Amuda, *aei* Amudavalli!' said a woman, addressing her friend across three 'leaves'. 'Did you have *morkuzhmbu*? It's A-1. Have some more, it's your favourite.'

'I will, Akka. Thanks for reminding me,' grinned Amuda.

Another man came with a small steel bucket of *koottu*. 'Anybody wants *koottu*? Come on all of you, eat shamelessly,' he repeated, encouraging them to eat without feeling shy. Two women smiled and started teasing him.

'Anne, do you help your wife in cooking, at your home?'

'What! *Ade*, what a question?' he chuckled, pausing for a minute with the utensils in his hand. 'Home is a different matter, why are you talking about home? Forget everything now and eat heartily.'

'Tell us, Anne. Isn't your wife a very lucky woman that she gets to be served by you?'

'Oh ho! You naughty women. Yes of course, she is lucky, but home is a different place,' he grinned.

Another woman said, 'Anne is very clever. He is dodging us. I bet he doesn't serve his wife at home. It is she who has to do that. Am I not right, Anne?'

'Stop gossiping and hurry. People are waiting outside for their turn. Shall I get you jackfruit and honey?' he said, turning to walk out of that row.

Again, there was a peal of laughter. One woman screamed above the din.

'You're a very good man, Anne. Really.'

Tara forgot the food on her leaf and watched in fascination. The warm banter between the women who gobbled up the food from their leaf and looked after the 'leaf' of their friends, and the men who served them generous helpings of whatever they wanted in a reversal of role—both of them seemed to have moved on to another stratosphere! The women looked so happy, and so did the men who put a smile on their faces.

Tara returned to herself when she heard the man say, 'Amma, let me get some fresh hot rice for you, and then curds.'

'All right.'

He came back with rice and curds that he served with *mormilagai*. He kept a small plastic cup and poured *payasam* into it. From another large steel bowl, he took out freshly peeled ripe jackfruit. Tara looked at the gold-hued fruit. Each one of them had an opening on the top. The man waited.

She looked at him, not knowing what she was supposed to do.

'Amma, won't you hold out your jackfruit for some honey? I'll pour some for you,' he said.

'Oh, yes. Sorry, I made you wait. Here, please pour the honey. This is fantastic!' said Tara. She had forgotten for a moment that Dorai mentioned jackfruit as part of the menu.

The man poured honey carefully into each one of the fruits on her leaf.

'Anything else, Amma?'

'Eh…no. Let me eat this first. I feel so full.'

'There's no hurry. Please take your time. Call one of us when you need something. We're all here,' he said and bustled over the next table. 'Who wants more *payasam* or jackfruit?' he asked, glancing at the row of women on the two tables.

Tara ate her jackfruit nervously, worried if some honey would dribble over her dress. There were no tissues around this place, but who cared? She pulled out another handkerchief from her handbag and sucked in the honey carefully. What a great combination, jackfruit and honey. She remembered Molly, her friend from Kerala who would often bring a delicious sweet prepared with jackfruit. After the routine school lunch with their mutual friends, the two of them would escape for 10 minutes to the playground at the rear portion of the school, find a shady place to sit and share the sweet in secret.

Tara's long hair was parted in the middle, plaited in two sections, then folded double and secured with satin ribbons on both sides of her head. She was eating at home with her siblings and cousins. Some honey had already dropped on to her school dress. Must wash it off before she left for school, she thought to herself. Also, she would have to brush her teeth to subdue the strong fragrance of jackfruit or else, she wouldn't be able to open her mouth to speak. People would instantly find out that she had eaten jackfruit. She'll tell her mother that from tomorrow, she would have jackfruit after she returns from school.

No time to compete with her cousins today. 'Four!' 'My score is seven', 'Eight!' boasted another.

'You'll get sick,' she warned, as the boys carried on nonchalantly, swallowing one fruit after another.

Through the window of the dining room, Tara could see the rear garden of their house. The banana tree laden with purple banana flowers, the tall, gnarled jackfruit tree that seemed to stand guard over the garden like an old, trusted caretaker. The fragrance of jasmine wafting above the plants, the heady smell from the marukkozhundu patch from the right side of the window…

'Hurry Tara, or you'll be late for school,' her mother was urging her to eat fast.

'Amma, shall I get you some more *payasam*? Did you like it?' asked the friendly waiter, pulling her back into the present.

'Thank you. It's very good and I've already had a lot. I'm full.'

'Then let me get you another tumbler of *neer mor*. It's a digestive. The ginger in it will make you feel better. And when you go out, please have *beeda* from the reception. Each one is wrapped with *thalir vetrilai*. It has *kraambu* which will also help in digestion,' he suggested. He offered a plate of *saunf* with small pieces of *kalkandu*.

She put some in her mouth and placed three 100 rupees notes on his plate.

'Amma! It's too much,' he protested.

'Sshh! Just take it. You transported me to my childhood today, even if it was for only one hour,' she smiled. And all of you have given a happy girls' day out for these women who slave in the kitchen every day, she thought, glancing over his shoulder to take one last look at the chattering women. Their voices rose above the din and clatter of waiters who walked up and down the aisles between the tables.

The man took the money with a smile and pressed his palms together. He accompanied her to the door. Dorai was waiting for her, his face a picture of consternation.

Tara beamed a smile at him and at the man who was now pointing at the *beeda* on the reception table. She paid for two, gave one to Dorai and walked out. It felt as if a great weight had slid off from her shoulders. She felt light on her feet. To think that she had re-lived her childhood in the most unlikely of places, and in a totally unexpected way...A bird fluttered its wings and flew out of her chest. As she walked out of the place, the chattering women in brightly coloured sarees floated behind her, their carefree laughter, the bangles tinkling on their arms, their faces lit up with mirth and mischievous jokes while they bonded over food and the serving waiters. Their mother Annapurni watched, waving a wand of bonhomie that wrapped around each one of them.

நெடுங்கதைகள்

Long Stories

JANAKI TURNS A BLIND EYE

[1]

The collective aroma of rice, wheat, jaggery, *ghee*, cooking oil, bananas, mangoes and other essentials pervaded the small *uggiranam*, the store room of the household. Janaki had gotten used to the smell in this poorly ventilated room where she spent most of her time sitting on a small cane chair. This was the only space she could claim as her own. It was also considered safe for her. Frail with age, and nearly blinded by acute diabetes that deteriorated with the utter neglect and absence of any medical treatment, she could only move within the house by groping around with her hands, negotiating her way slowly by holding on to walls, doors and familiar objects to avoid colliding with people. For that matter, nobody in the large family had a room of their own in the modest house that had just three small rooms for her widowed daughter Alamelu and her large brood of grown up children. At night, all the women huddled in one room to sleep, the men in another room, while Janaki and Alamelu slept in the third room along with the younger siblings.

Ironically, it was the small *uggiranam* that gave some privacy to the women of the household. On the pretext of taking out things for their daily cooking, women also used the room to whisper about family gossip, share secrets and occasionally change their sarees.

When her legs stiffened due to sitting, Janaki would venture out of this stifling room to the front courtyard to feel the warmth of sunlight on her body. Her eldest grandson Krishnan (Kittu to the family) and Alamelu would be there, chatting, planning, executing their various strategies for coping with the material needs of their large family. Janaki would settle in a far corner, close her rheumy eyes and doze off. Once she closed her eyes, she could always hear Alamelu and Kittu more clearly. Strange! In proportion to her loss of vision, her hearing capacity seemed to have increased manifold times. She often wondered why. If she wanted sunlight, she had to listen to their talk and that often put her off. It was driven by selfishness, greed and an unscrupulous opportunism.

'Up till now, the boy's side have agreed to most of our arrangements for Shanta's wedding,' said Alamelu, mother of the bride-to-be. 'I explained that I lost my husband some years back and have to manage a large family. Still, they dropped hints that I should give enough jewellery, silverware and *javali* for all the important members of their family. Where will we go for all that? We have two more daughters to be married,' said a worried Alamelu.

'Don't worry, Amma,' said Krishnan. 'We'll manage.'

'But how? Our budget is already stretched and there's simply no money left to invest in jewellery and silver,' said Alamelu, keeping her voice low.

'There's the new bride, Vidya,' said Krishnan. 'Her parents have loaded her with lots of good, chunky jewellery and strands of gold chains, bangles and bracelets. She also brought a lot of silverware, even though we didn't ask for it. A rose-water sprinkler, large carved cups for sandal paste, turmeric and *kumkum*, silver *puja* plates, a pair of tall silver *kuttu vilakku*. Amma, she even had some silver containers with lids,' he laughed. 'I casually asked her father what they were for. He said, "Our Vidya is emotionally attached to them. She'll use them in whichever way she wants—to keep earrings or trinkets. They're her *streedhan* given fondly by her mother," he smiled indulgently. 'Imagine, keeping earrings in a silver container!' chuckled Krishnan, in a sarcastic tone.

'Vidya comes from a well-to-do family, but why are you talking about it now?' asked Alamelu.

'Amma, have you forgotten what I did to bride no. 2, Padmaja? Remember how I made her *puli-nagam*, the tiger-claw necklace disappear, along with her silver lamps some years back?'

'Oh yes, I remember now,' said Alamelu.

'It was a double tiger-claw mounted on gold, a heavy pendant on a heavy necklace that fetched us a good amount of money. Padmaja was very upset, because the tiger-claw was supposed to act as a charm to protect her against malevolent spirits. Little did she know that I was one such spirit! Her health was poorly,' exulted Krishnan, laughing.

'You pulled it off somehow,' said Alamelu.

'Of course, I did. The fool searched for it frantically and I too joined in the search!' he chuckled loudly. Alamelu laughed with him.

'I told Padmaja I'm very sorry she lost it, but I also scolded her. "You should've been more careful. When there's a wedding in the family, the house will naturally swarm with servants. You lost it because of your carelessness!" I said.'

'Okay, do something like that, Kittu. But act fast! The wedding is fast approaching,' said Alamelu.

'Leave it to me,' said Krishnan. The two of them were silent for a while.

Janaki stirred in her cemented seat and got up.

'Are you going in, Amma?' asked Alamelu. 'Be careful. Hold on to the walls.'

'Don't worry. I'll be fine,' said Janaki, going past the front door. She reached the store room and sat on her cane chair, fighting the sense of disgust that engulfed her.

***

[2]

There were some footfalls.

'Who is there? Is it Vidya?' Janaki could discern a slim figure in a blur.

'Yes, Patti. You're amazing! How could you tell it's me?' Vidya was just getting used to Janaki's uncanny ability to identify footfalls despite her severely impaired vision.

'Your footfalls are also soft and cultured like you, that's why,' smiled Janaki. 'Do you know why I keep my eyes closed most of the time?'

'Why, Patti?'

'So that I can hear better.'

'What!' laughed Vidya.

'Yes, girl! When I keep my eyes closed, what people say is far clearer than it would be otherwise,' she remarked, smiling again.

'Really? How can that be?' asked Vidya. 'Patti, I came in to get some *besan*. The container is right here. You please sit comfortably where you are.'

Such a refined girl, comes from a decent family. Is always polite to elders. She is educated, unlike her other sisters-in-law, who haven't been to college or even to high school. She is in a good job too, I heard, ruminated Janaki.

'Ah, got it,' said Vidya. 'Do you want something, Patti?

Coffee or may be a glass of buttermilk with some crushed ginger, salt and curry leaves?' she asked.

'I would like some buttermilk, but first you must listen to what I have to say. I need to talk to you about something urgent,' said Janaki.

'Why? What's the matter?' asked Vidya.

'Bolt the door.'

'Oh no, Patti! Somebody will surely knock on it. We're always in and out of this room to take things for cooking,' said Vidya.

'Never mind. If somebody knocks, tell her that you're changing your saree. Now bolt the door! I told you it's urgent,' she whispered.

Vidya bolted the door.

'Listen. What I'm about to tell you is very important,' said Janaki in a hushed voice. Vidya bent over close to listen.

'For your sister-in-law Shanti's upcoming wedding, my grandson Krishnan, who you call Periya Anna, is plotting to steal your jewellery, silverware, may be even your silk sarees. Don't take any of them out of your suitcase. Keep them locked at all times and hide the key safely somewhere, may be inside your handbag. Sleep with the handbag under your pillow. And if you go out, take the handbag with you,' said Janaki.

'What!' Vidya was beside herself with shock.

'*Issh*! Speak in whispers,' warned Janaki 'I heard the plan yesterday. Kittu stole the jewellery of your elder sister-in-law

Padmaja too. Poor woman, how distraught she was, searching for her *puli-nagam* necklace in vain! Now he plans to steal much more from you, because your parents gave you a lot.'

Vidya went near Janaki and gently held her hand. Is Patti hallucinating? All day she sits in a corner. Nobody talks to her. Is she imagining things? she wondered.

'Patti, why're you talking like this?' whispered Vidya in her ears, softly.

'It's true! I heard them plotting and planning last evening. I'm warning you because I've seen this happen before. It's disgusting. Oh, I wish I die soon!' said Janaki, looking very agitated.

'All right Patti, all right,' said Vidya, patting her hand. 'I'll do as you say. Oh my god!' said Vidya, in utter disbelief.

'*Issh*! Don't raise your voice. You don't know that man. He is a smooth swindler, utterly cunning and unscrupulous. I'm ashamed to say that my daughter Alamelu is a partner in his crimes. His wife Priya is also hand in glove with him. She'll do whatever Kittu commands her to do because she has nowhere to go. Comes from a poor family, has no father. I'm telling you for your own good. Or else, why will I risk my neck to tell you?' said Janaki. Her voice turned husky with the effort of keeping it low. Her slender shoulders shook with rage.

Vidya went numb with shock. It was true that she got married to a family that was in many ways lower in status than hers—economically, socially and even in their education level. Some of her brothers-in-law were average men in clerical jobs with government offices and private firms. Her sisters-in-law were school dropouts.

Vidya came close to Janaki and stroked her cheeks softly. There was a knock on the door. Janaki signalled to Vidya, to say something.

'Who is it? Just a minute. I'm rearranging my sari. The string of my skirt snapped.'

'Okay,' replied the woman outside. Must be the third daughter-in-law.

Janaki resumed her whisper. 'Listen, girl. Do as I tell you. Act fast! Or else you'll regret it. Understand?'

'Yes...yes, Patti. Now let me go and get you buttermilk.'

'All right, go. Remember to be firm, always. Just pretend that you don't know where you've misplaced the keys to your box. If they insist, ask them point blank "Why do you need it?" Tell them you can very well wear the nice Kanjeevaram silk sarees you wore, when you arrived from Chennai. Don't open your suitcase, use your daily clothes from your big handbag.'

Vidya was surprised at the precision of Janaki's observations. Is she the one who has gone blind or is it me who is really blind, with my eyes open? Janaki placed her hand on her head, 'Go, may God bless you', she whispered.

There was another knock. 'Vidya, have you finished wearing your saree? I want to get something,' said daughter in law no. 3.

'Yes *Manni*, in a minute', said Vidya, and opened the door. She smiled at the woman and showed her the container of *besan*. 'Okay, hurry up. Amma is waiting for you,' said the woman, reaching for cooking oil. She glanced briefly at Janaki who was apparently asleep, curled up on her cane chair.

Vidya returned with a cool glass of buttermilk.

'Patti, please have this buttermilk.'

Janaki sat up and drained her glass gratefully. 'May you live long and happily as a *sumangali* with our dear Chandru,' she blessed Vidya.

***

[3]

Vidya glanced at her two sisters-in-law sleeping in the room. Priya Manni would be coming in late, and Padmaja was yet to arrive for the wedding. Vidya placed her handbag under her pillow and closed her eyes. What a weird thing she had heard, it sounded so improbable! But Patti was in dead earnest. Patti, so frail in her health, compounded by her impaired vision, looks like she'll leave this world any moment. Yet, she champions for the 'right' things like she has a mission and exerts with all her dwindling strength to protect me.

How can anyone steal from family members? Shall I go out on some pretext tomorrow and call my mother? But somebody is sure to tag along and report that I made a call from a phone outside the home. It's a large family that just doesn't have any concept of privacy. No one seeks it, no one gets it. All of them snoop around. Vidya tossed on the mattress sleeplessly. If she can't call her parents, she certainly can't call her husband Chandrashekar either, who is now in Berlin, Germany, doing a course. Let him work in peace. Someone will definitely accompany her to the place from where one made international calls. Kittu Anna, who is planning all this, may himself accompany her to see if she was 'complaining' about anything. No, no, that'll spoil all the chance of safeguarding her jewellery and silver. I must go by the advice of Janaki Patti. There's something extraordinary about her. Just look at her stand-alone spirit! She is frail, but has a strong political will, resisting an unethical action. I respect that.

Vidya looked at her sisters-in-law, oblivious of any threat to their personal belongings. Both of them came from small towns. No, one of them was from a village. Sleep eluded her. She recalled the letter her father had received from Kittu Anna. It was so flattering! 'Your daughter Vidya has brought us luck. The minute she stepped into our house, our Chandru got an invite from Berlin for this UNESCO sponsored course! Next, Shanta's wedding got finalised. I understand that you'll be going to Delhi to work with your colleagues because the Parliament would be in session and that your wife is also accompanying you. At least, kindly send Vidya for the marriage'. Vidya's mother Sudha also got a similar letter written in Tamil from her mother-in-law Alamelu, gushing about the good luck ushered by Vidya. She said at least Vidya should come to fill in the absence of Chandru.

After that, Sudha got a call from Priya, saccharine sweet in tone. 'How beautiful Vidya looked during her marriage, in the jewellery you had so tastefully made for her. And such a nice selection of Kanjeevaram sarees too, not one bit gaudy. Pity we were all busy managing our big family. We didn't even get the time to see her properly. Now we want to show her off to the in-laws of Shanta,' she laughed. 'So, please let her come with at least some of her jewellery and the sarees. We'll take good care of them.' Sudha was completely charmed. Both she and her husband came from families that were quiet and reticent, not given to much gushing. 'Certainly, certainly,' agreed Sudha. Along with some of her heavy, stone-set jewellery, diamond earrings and bracelet, Sudha packed, on a last-minute impulse, the carved silver bowls for sandal paste, turmeric, *kumkum* and *kalkandu*, the traditional rock sugar, to welcome wedding guests. 'I doubt if this family has enough silver. But remember! You should only dry-clean them with a soft cloth after use. Pack them back carefully. Don't be careless,' she had advised.

Vidya took a flight from Chennai to Tiruchi so that she can rush back on time for her office commitments.

***

Vidya recalled the discussions her parents had before she married Chandru. 'It's a large family. Chandrashekar doesn't have a father. Still, your father and I liked them for so readily agreeing to let you continue your work at office, whether you're transferred to another city or not. That's rather unusual. Even some rich or upper middle-class families are so rigid in the name of convention, tradition and what not. Some go the extent of asking a girl outright to give up her job, soon after her marriage. Imagine, after all the education and training!'

'Yes, Amma. I've seen that happening to my friends,' said Vidya.

And now, there is this seismic wave set in motion by our frail Janaki Patti who can't see anything beyond a foot. How come Janaki Patti's hearing is so sharp? Will this Kittu Anna stoop so low as to steal jewellery and silver from brides who come into their family? She closed her eyes and tried to sleep. Images floated vividly within her eyes.

Her mother Sudha rushing through her work for the day so that she could visit the family goldsmith to check on her custom-made order for Vidya's necklace, bracelet, earrings set with sparkling Blue Jager diamonds. The entire extended family praised Sudha for her exquisite taste in designing the jewellery for Vidya and the carved silver ware.

Like her peers, Vidya wore minimal jewellery to office. Only on festive occasions at home or to weddings, she wore the jewellery given by her mother. Her mind flooded with fond memories of her mother and her delight in seeing the jewellery on her daughter.

'Amma, Appa, I'll save my jewellery and silverware, come what may! They're your loving gifts to me. I won't let this cunning man steal them. What he is doing is grossly wrong. Not just for me, but for every woman. I'll put an end to it', she told herself.

***

There was a flurry of activity for Shanta's upcoming *Sumangali Prarthanai*, an event done ahead of the wedding. Two cooks were hired to manage the elaborate lunch for the family and the guests. The store room was packed to capacity with the extra grocery bought for the occasion. Women walked in and out of the room all day long either to keep or take something. Janaki went out of the room for some fresh air.

Since the front courtyard was crowded with Krishnan and male visitors, she slowly made her way to the backyard.

The day's laundry was done. Janaki spread her towel on the washing stone and sat on it. The breeze blowing from the mango tree felt soft and silky on her limbs. Janaki closed her eyes.

'Ah, there you are, Vidya.'

This is Priya, Kittu's wife.

'I'm putting out the clothes to dry, Manni,' replied Vidya. 'Will be done in five minutes.'

'Take your time. Just came to remind you to wear your lovely jewellery for *Sumangali Prarthanai*. After all, you're a newly-wed girl,' smiled Priya.

'Oh Manni, but I shouldn't out-shine the bride Shanta,' laughed Vidya.

'Don't be silly! I knew you would say something like that. You educated, working girls are all alike. Don't like to wear jewellery. But *Sumangali Prarthanai* is a festive celebration. You should be dressed appropriately.'

'Sure, Manni,' said Vidya.

'Okay. Now I must go in to supervise the cooks,' said Priya and went inside.

Perched on the washing stone, Janaki Patti flashed a smile at Vidya. Has she gone in? She gestured. Vidya walked over to where she sat and whispered 'Yes Patti, she has gone in. Don't worry, I'll do exactly like you advised. Now let me walk you back into the house.'

She held Janaki's hand till they reached the back door. Janaki shook her hand free so that no one will see them come in together. Then she slowly went inside, holding on to the walls. Such a model of tact and discretion, our Patti, marvelled Vidya.

***

For *Sumangali Prarthanai* Vidya changed into a nice Kanjeevaram saree that she had worn on the first day of her arrival from Chennai. She didn't wear any extra jewellery.

'Vidya, I asked you to wear your jewellery,' said Priya. 'Put on your diamond earrings. Your lovely emerald-and-pearl necklace would go with this saree. You shouldn't have an 'everyday' look on this occasion,' she added.

Vidya lowered her voice and said, 'Oh Manni, I don't know how to tell you. I can't find the keys to my suitcase. I searched everywhere, but let's not disturb this auspicious event'.

'Goodness! Where did you misplace it?' said Priya. 'Don't worry, we'll search for you, as soon as we get some free time.'

'Oh, thanks so much, Manni! How very kind of you. Thank God I at least have this Kanjeevaram saree to save my face.'

The *Sumangali Prarthanai* went off reasonably well.

***

[4]

'Ah, I'm sorry,' said a male voice.

Vidya tuned around to face Krishnan standing on the doorway, his face placid. 'I heard from Priya that you couldn't find the keys to your suitcase.'

'That's all right, Periya Anna. I'll search again. I'm sure I'll find it, please don't bother anymore about it,' said Vidya.

'But you'll need the jewellery and sarees soon, for the wedding. Shall I arrange for a locksmith to break it open? We'll have a new one replaced. I know a good person who can do it,' he said pleasantly, as if he offered to help her mend a broken umbrella.

'Oh no, Anna. No need to take such extreme measures. Let me search once more for the key'.

'Anyway, give it a thought,' he shrugged, his jaw set hard as he left the room.

***

Janaki reclined on a chair at the far end of the front courtyard, her eyes tightly closed. She could smell coffee being served to Krishnan and Alamelu by somebody.

'Amma, your new daughter-in-law Vidya is one stubborn girl. I offered to get her a locksmith to open her suitcase, because she needs the jewels for the wedding. She refused point blank,' said Krishnan.

'Really?'

'Yes. She said she'll search for the key once again.'

'Kittu, shall we go ahead and break it open, whether she likes it or not?'

'I had half a mind to do that, but it's very dicey. You see, if we break it open without her consent, and then she finds out that her jewellery or silverware is missing, it'll arouse her suspicion.'

'Hmm…So what shall we do now?' asked Alamelu.

'I'm really perplexed,' said Krishnan. 'All I want now is to get even with this girl, show her what I'm made off. Damn!' he swore under his breath. 'Anyway, we've got her huge brass and copper containers that she brought with her when she came as a bride, loaded with sweets and snacks, remember?'

'I do. So, what do you propose to do?' asked Alamelu.

'It's already done! I fixed up the vessel marker to come exactly during that post-lunch time when your upper-class Vidya has her beauty sleep with the other daughters-in-law. He cleverly erased the initials 'VC' for Vidya Chandrashekar and imprinted Shanta's name in a larger lettering. He is such an expert that you can't even tell! With his help, we put away the containers in the attic over the kitchen. Vidya is so preoccupied that she didn't even look for them,' he gloated, with a dry laugh.

'Good work, Kittu! Otherwise, those huge containers cost a fortune now. They seem to be her mother's, for you can't even get them now,' said Alamelu.

'And now they're are Shanta's,' he chuckled, very pleased with his cunning strategies. 'Her mother-in-law will be pleased that we gave her wedding sweets and snacks in these rare containers. Still, I'm really perplexed about missing out on the jewels,' continued Krishnan, swearing under his breath.

They talked of various other things for some time. Alamelu got up and went near Janaki.

'Amma, get up. It's time you ate dinner and went to bed,' she said, lightly touching her shoulders.

Janaki slowly opened her eyes. 'Is it night already?' she asked Alamelu laughed. 'What's the matter? These days you can't make out whether it is day or night. Come, hold on to me,' she said, walking her back to the house.

***

Shanta's wedding was a simple affair. After she was sent off, the men in the household got busy making train bookings for the rest of the family who had to return to their respective places.

'So many bookings are wait-listed. I could get a confirmed booking only on a night train to Chennai,' declared Krishnan to Vidya. 'If you wait for a few more days, I can get a day train,' he added, smoothly.

'Doesn't matter, Periya Anna. Thanks so much for all the trouble. If you can please book me on a ladies' compartment, that would be nice,' said Vidya.

'Okay. But why don't you stay back for a few more days and help in tidying up all this chaos after the wedding?' said Krishnan.

'I would've loved to, but I've to return and relieve another person who has applied for leave. Also, some important meetings have been scheduled with our clients,' explained Vidya.

'Why don't you take a flight, in that case? After all, you came by flight?' he asked testily, knowing fully well that she couldn't. It would entail opening the suitcase to transfer all the jewellery and silver ware to her cabin luggage.

'No Anna, the night train in a women's compartment will be just fine for me,' said Vidya, moving out of the room.

***

Janaki slowly made her way to the front courtyard and sat at some distance from Alamelu, Krishnan, and his wife Priya.

'Amma, stretch yourself comfortably on that wooden bench at the far corner,' said Alamelu.

Janaki moved toward the bench.

'Your great, upper-class Vidya, the high-born *peri idatthu penn* is leaving for Chennai tomorrow,' said Krishnan to his mother.

'I know,' replied Alamelu. 'It seems you could get a reservation only on a night train. Are you sending someone with her, Venkat or Srini?'

'No!' said Krishnan, raising his voice. 'Let it be a punishment for this so-called emancipated woman, ha! If she wants freedom, this is how she gets it,' he laughed in a harsh tone. 'I asked her to stay back and help in tidying up. But she refused saying she has important meetings. Humph! These office-going women are the limit,' he said, gnashing his teeth.

'So, she'll travel alone on the night train, with all that jewellery in her suitcase? What if her parents object to the way we've sent her, without an escort?' asked Alamelu

'Let them object, who cares? That's the way to treat her, the clever witch,' chipped in Priya. 'How she put on a cunning act, saying she misplaced her key to the suitcase, that she couldn't find it and so on…All as a ruse so that no one can reach for her jewellery,' said Priya, keeping her voice low.

'Just look at the way she was dressed on the day of the wedding. A simple Kanjeevaram saree with nothing around her neck except her *thaali*, the *mangal sutra*, as if her mother didn't give her anything,' fumed Alamelu.

'I had planned to take her stone-set necklace, the matching earrings and bangles, and give them to Shanta later, for her *thalai Deepavali* or *thalai Pongal.* She spoilt everything for me,' said Krishnan, cursing under his breath.

'Such a proud girl! All that education and her job has gone to her head,' muttered Alamelu. 'You know, I asked Chandru why he chose to marry this girl who works in an office but he said he had made up his mind. He even went so far as to say that he couldn't believe that she and her parents agreed to this match, considering the fact that we're not equal to her, socially or economically.'

'How dare he say that, Amma?' said Krishnan.

'Well, he did,' Alamelu replied.

'Let her go alone by the night train with all that goddam jewellery. That'll teach her a lesson,' he said.

All of them sat in silence for a long time.

There was a rustling sound. Janaki had got up.

'Priya, help Amma get inside the house. It's dark,' said Alamelu.

'Come, Patti. I'll help you walk back,' said Priya, holding her hand.

***

[5]

'Patti, *namaskaram*. I'm leaving for Chennai late in the evening,' said Vidya, touching her feet in the store room.

Janaki placed her hand on Vidya's head. 'Wish you a safe journey, dear child. May you rise in your career. May all the Gods that I have prayed to protect you during this night journey. Take care and give my regards to your parents. God bless you all,' said Janaki.

'Thank you, dearest Patti. I'll never forget what you've done for me. You've been like a guardian angel to me. I'm so grateful. *Nanri*, Patti. *Nanri*,' said Vidya, hugging Janaki's frail body.

'My dear child, I could only save your jewellery, not the solid big brass and copper containers that you brought, during your wedding.'

'Why, what about them?' asked Vidya.

'*Issh*! Speak in whispers. Kittu has taken them for Shanta, by erasing your initials on the containers and imprinting Shanta's name in a larger lettering.'

'Oh my God!' whispered Vidya, holding Janaki's hand. 'I never knew. In fact, I didn't even see those huge containers this time.'

'How could you, dear girl? They are stashed away in the attic over the kitchen, away from your sight. May he rot in hell, Kittu and the whole lot of the thieving people in this house.'

Janaki's thin body trembled. Vidya hugged her and stroked her back. 'It's all right, Patti, please don't get so upset. What's gone is gone. You take care of yourself. You're the purest soul here.' Vidya touched her feet once again, kissed her brow and left.

The rest of the family gave Vidya a cold send-off. She retaliated silently by refusing to eat anything. One of her sisters-in-law felt sorry for her and furtively packed some *puris* with spiced potatoes for Vidya. 'Have it on the train,' she whispered. A younger brother-in-law accompanied her to the train station only to help her get settled in her coach. He waved his hand at her perfunctorily and left before the train started.

When the train moved, Vidya noticed the other two women in the compartment. One of them was adjusting her boxes and bags. The other woman was young and looked like a nun. She was dressed all in white except for a grey tunic and was saying the rosary. Let me talk to her after she finishes her prayers, thought Vidya, pulling out her own prayer book. Softly, she recited the Tamil *shlokas* for Lord Krishna, her favourite deity. Help me Krishna, protect me, protect all three of us in this night train, she prayed.

Once she got to know that Krishnan had no intention of sending any of his brothers to escort her back on this night train, she had insisted on a women's compartment. I have the blessings of Janaki Patti, she told herself. She caught the young nun looking at her as she pushed the suitcase further inside.

The nun crossed herself, kissed the cross dangling on her chain, replaced her prayer book and smiled at Vidya, who smiled back at her.

'Going up to Chennai?' she asked.

'Yes, Sister. May I call you Sister?' asked Vidya.

'But of course!' she replied, smiling broadly. 'I'm Mary Sebastian. You can also call me Mary,' she said.

'I'm Vidya.'

The third woman was having her dinner from her tiffin box.

'Have you brought something to eat?' asked Sister Mary.

'Yes. Will you have some *puri*s with potato?' offered Vidya.

'No, thanks,' said Sister Mary. 'I've brought my dinner.' She opened her tiffin box. 'What brought you to Tiruchy?' she inquired.

'My sister-in-law's wedding,' said Chandra.

'Sister-in-law! Why, you don't even look married! You look like a college girl, *pullae*. When did you get married?' smiled Sister Mary.

'Three months back.'

'Why are you travelling alone, pullae? Didn't your husband come for his sister's wedding?'

'He is in Berlin, Germany, training in a course. And my parents were not free.'

'I see.'

The third woman finished her dinner, washed her hands and returned to settle down to sleep. Vidya felt her eyelids drooping with fatigue. No, I mustn't sleep, I must keep awake and look after my suitcase, she told herself. Both Mary and Vidya washed their hands and returned to their seats. Mary took out a book and got immersed in reading.

Vidya also had a book but couldn't concentrate. The train pulled up at a small station. What if I fall asleep and some people get into the compartment and walk away with my suitcase, she thought, fear gripping her. After all the trouble that Janaki Patti went into, and my play-acting about the 'lost key', would I lose my things to a common thief? Now I must fight this sleep that's engulfing me. Vidya turned the pages of her book.

***

'Vidya, here's your book. It had dropped down to the floor. Stretch yourself on the berth and sleep properly,' said Sister Mary. Vidya got up, very embarrassed.

'Oh, thank you so much, Sister. Guess I just dozed off. A wedding can be very tiring,' explained Vidya.

'I know. But it's time to sleep anyway,' smiled Sister Mary.

'Aren't you sleepy yet, Sister?' asked Chandra.

'I'll sleep in a while. Just want to read a few more pages.'

'Sister.'

'Yes, pullae?'

'That lady is fast asleep. If the two of us also go to sleep, won't somebody come into this compartment and...'

Sister Mary immediately got up and fastened the latch on the doors, on both sides of the compartment.

'There. Now nobody can come.'

'But...you see, there's a fourth berth up there? Someone may get in from another station. Then we'll have to open the door,' said Vidya.

'Sure, we'll open when the fourth woman comes. Until then we'll keep it bolted for our safety. Who knows, may be there'll be no fourth woman,' said Sister Mary, returning calmly to her book.

Vidya stretched herself on her berth. Cradled by the rhythmic movement and sounds of the train, she was lulled into a deep sleep. Suddenly, the train jerked into a screeching halt. She sat up to see the name of the station, but it was pitch dark outside. The train had stopped in the middle of a wilderness. Sister Mary was awake. 'Wonder why it has stopped?' she said aloud. 'Somebody must've pulled a chain.'

Vidya got up to check the doors. They were firmly latched on both sides. Then she bent down to glance at her suitcase under the berth. Sister Mary smiled at her reassuringly. 'Don't worry. I'll keep an eye on your suitcase. I know it must be packed with jewels and wedding sarees.'

Vidya smiled back nervously. She pushed her suitcase further inside so that it wouldn't be visible for anybody.

'Where is your suitcase, Sister?' asked Vidya.

'I don't have one, pullae. I just brought two large bags, that's all,' she replied.

How nice to be a nun, thought Vidya. No excess baggage to carry. The train started slowly crawling out of the station. Hope it'll only stop at proper train stations and not at some godforsaken place, she thought. Sleep claimed her once again.

Whenever the train jolted a bit on its way, Vidya woke up drowsily only to find Sister Mary reclining, looking out of the window, and praying with her rosary.

'Sister, please go to sleep,' said Vidya. 'I'll stay awake for some time and keep an eye on our things.' Mary Sebastian smiled at her genially and said, 'Just go to sleep, pullae. You must be very tired after the wedding activities. I want to read this book for some more time.'

Vidya's tired body rocked along with the moving train. From her half-closed eyes, she saw Sister Mary, luminous in her white and grey dress, with her book resting on her lap. She looks like an angel, thought Vidya. Don't angels feel sleepy?

***

There were some noises now. The train slowed down and stopped. Sunlight streamed in through their glass-shuttered windows. Ah, it's morning. Sister Mary was nowhere around. Panic gripped Vidya. Instinctively, she glanced down under her berth. The suitcase was there. She sprang up from her berth to check the doors. The latch was firmly in place on both sides of the compartment. The third woman was still asleep. So, there was no fourth woman. But where is Sister Mary?

'Good morning,' she said, emerging from the washroom.

'A very good morning to you, Sister. I'll also brush and wash. Then we can have some coffee.'

It was a big station with vendors screaming 'Coffee, tea, newspapers.'

Vidya brushed hurriedly and bought two coffees. She handed one over to Sister Mary.

'Thank you. May I pay you for this?' asked Sister Mary.

'No, of course not!' smiled Vidya. 'It's my pleasure, entirely. Just let's enjoy the coffee.'

'Hmm...' said Sister Mary, sipping the steaming cup appreciatively. 'It's good coffee!' she remarked.

'Would you like another cup, Sister?' asked Vidya.

'Would love it,' she smiled.

Vidya got two more cups of coffee. Sister Mary drank hers eagerly. They glanced out of the windows. More well-lit stations could be seen.

'We'll be in Chennai very soon,' said Vidya.

'Yes,' replied the Sister Mary, lowering her voice. 'Good, this lady has also woken up.'

'It's also good that the fourth woman never came, and we didn't have to unbolt the door in the middle of the night,' said Vidya.

'Which fourth woman?' asked Sister Mary.

'Remember? I said this compartment is for four people and a fourth woman may come when we're sleeping?' said Vidya.

'Oh yes, now I remember. Perhaps she came invisibly, to keep a vigil on us. Because we're three women on a night train, with a valuable suitcase under your berth,' smiled Sister Mary, with a mischievous twinkle in her eye.

'Invisibly?' laughed Vidya. If so, then the fourth woman must be my dear Janaki Patti, she thought.

'Who knows, pullae? The Lord Jesus brings about many silent miracles. Maybe He came in the guise of that invisible fourth woman to protect us and our belongings,' she said, her smile broadening into a grin now.

Vidya looked at her, stupefied. Sister Mary however was in a mirthful mood.

'I wouldn't be surprised, Vidya. The way I pestered Lord Jesus throughout the night, praying, asking Him to protect us, protect the precious suitcase. He must've thought, oh ho!

This Sister Mary is such a pest. Let me do the needful, or she won't allow me to be at peace. So, He must've come as the fourth invisible woman and protected us,' she laughed merrily, bending down to kiss the cross dangling over her tunic.

'Ah, here's Chennai,' she said, looking out of the window. She got up with her two bags.

'Appa, Amma,' cried out Vidya, spotting them outside the window. A porter got her suitcase out. She clasped Sister Mary by her hand and took her to her parents.

'This is Sister Mary Sebastian. But for her, I would've felt very, very scared,' said Vidya.

'Why, what happened Vidya?' asked her father. 'Why are you in a ladies' compartment? Is your brother-in-law in another compartment? We'll wait for him.'

'No. I came alone.'

'Alone? In a night train? But why? Surely one of Chandru's brothers could've come with you?' asked her father, his face flushed with anger.

'It's all right, Appa. Janaki Patti and Lord Jesus must've been with us in spirit, to look after all three of us. I'm most grateful to Sister Mary. She didn't sleep a wink throughout the night. She just sat up and prayed, keeping awake to look after us and our belongings,' said Vidya.

'Janaki Patti was with you in spirit? What're you saying, Vidya?' asked her mother Sudha, bewildered.

Vidya's father turned toward Sister Mary with folded hands. 'Thanks very much indeed, Madam,' he said.

Her mother placed her hand on Sister Mary's head, 'Dear child, may God bless you with a long life and eternal happiness. Are you allowed to visit people? Then please come to our house and have lunch with us someday.'

Sister Mary smiled back at them. 'I'll certainly come Aunty, Uncle. Thanks so much for the invite.' She folded her hands in a namaste and said 'May the Lord Jesus keep you all within His fold and protect you at all times.' She hugged Vidya. 'Take care, sweet pullae. Good bye.'

Turning to her left, she waved her hand at the two Sisters who had come to receive her. They were dressed just like her. One of them took her bags. Sister Mary smiled again at Vidya, with the same twinkle in her eyes. She bowed to her parents and melted into the crowd.

VRS

[1]

Arundhati drove in through the gate and parked the car in front of her house in the space allotted for her. When she went in, she saw Rooprani standing on the porch to take her bags and parcels from her.

'Has Doctor *Saab* come?' asked Arundhati.

'He came and went out again, Madam-ji. For a prayer meeting, he said. I gave him tea with snacks,' she replied.

'Ah…that's good. Now get a pot of hot tea to my room, Roop.'

'In a minute, Madam-ji.'

Arundhati washed her face, hands and feet, changed into a loose *kurta* over her *salwar* and settled down on a lounge chair in her room. It was just another day in the university, but she felt very tired. OA, as osteoarthritis was breezily called, had caught up with her and a few of her female colleagues. It's a tricky thing. One can't rest the aching legs for long, because movement was very important. Rest and OA don't go down well together.

Hence, osteoarthritis called for more physical work. One has to constantly move the legs, knees, arms, hips, and walk as much as one can. She had signed up for physiotherapy when the pain had gotten too severe. Even just sitting for long stiffened her legs. The half an hour or forty-five minutes' drive from work to home had to be compensated with stretches. After tea, she'll walk around the house and the small garden to remove the stiffness.

Thank God I got it later than others, she thought. During her first visit to the orthopaedic, he comforted her by saying that OA 'has gotten younger', which in medical parlance meant, now even people in their thirties and forties were getting this problem. The main snag is work didn't leave much time for exercise. Mornings are spent in a hurry to leave for the university on time, and in the evening one is too tired to walk or exercise. Even driving is getting to me, she thought, sipping her tea. Friends and colleagues had offered to help her find a good driver. True, drivers are expensive but worth the cost if she got some time to read for the *Gita* class that held regular meetings at Chinmaya Mission. Some of the speakers exuded a positive energy that revitalized her. Then there was another nascent group that got together, calling themselves modestly as the Gargi Group (GG). It was still a fledgling association that had to be developed as a registered body. They met occasionally whenever the Group invited erudite speakers who could talk about Maitreyi, Yajnavalkya and Gargi in the context of the Upanishads. GG was yet to evolve. She met some interesting people in both the places. A suggestion to link GG to the department of Philosophy at Delhi University was countered by many members who said it would lapse into a theoretical, academic set-up. They were keen to acquire knowledge that would help them engage with their lives more purposefully, like the *Gita* class tried to do. However, suggestions to invite eminent visiting scholars from the faculty of the department of Comparative Religion at Harvard University, or the Centre for Comparative Religions and Civilizations from the Central University of Jammu or distinguished speakers from Max Mueller Bhavan were welcomed enthusiastically by the members.

Arundhati poured herself anther hot cup of *elaichi* flavoured tea and bit into the crisp *namak para* and *mathri*. Nice woman, Roop. Such a good cook too. She mulled over some of the men recommended by her friends for a driver's job. She would shortlist a few who came with reliable references, and arrange to meet each one of them separately with Rajaraman. He didn't show much interest in hiring a driver, but Arundhati wanted to use the time spent in the car to catch up on reading or just rest her limbs. She had met Ramya, Vibha and her husband Sandeep Kaushik in a *Gita* class and was impressed with the way they earnestly studied the recommended books and joined actively in the discussions. She replaced the cup on the tray when she overheard some voices. Rooprani was talking to someone in an uncharacteristically raised voice. Arundhati went to the porch. It was Ramu, one of the security guards in their Residents Association.

'Yes, Ramu?'

'Namaste Madam-ji. I just came to keep some *khaad* that the maali had asked me to buy for your garden. This leafy *khaad* is sold by someone near our house,' he said.

'Where is the *khaad*?' asked Arundhati.

'Over there, Madam-ji. I kept it behind the jasmine bush so that birds don't scatter the contents. The *maali* asked me to keep it there.'

'Okay then.'

'Hey Ramu, close the gate when you go,' snapped Rooprani. 'And the next time you come, ring the bell or knock on the door to let me know you're here.'

'Arre Roop, don't make such a noise about it,' Ramu said cheekily.

'Don't you Roop me! Just don't sneak in, that's all,' she said, leaving the portico in a huff.

Arundhati returned to her room, showered and sat down to shortlist the names for drivers. She ticked two of them. One of them had worked for her friend for a long time till she left Delhi, and the other one was known to her cousin's family. The aroma of roasted *jeera* and *dhania* wafted from the kitchen. Let me read a little bit for the Gargi Group before it's time for dinner, she thought, settling down on the lounge chair. She could hear the gate opening. Must be Raj. She read the book on her lap even as she waited indefinitely for her husband. What's taking him so long? She tried to read a few more pages, then closed the book with a bookmark and went to the porch.

Rajaraman was standing near the jasmine bush.

'Taking a walk?'

'Just a short stroll, Dattie. Good that you're back,' he smiled.

'Want some more tea?'

'Don't mind another cup, actually,' he nodded.

'Come inside then,' she said.

Arundhati went to the kitchen to ask Rooprani to make a cup of tea for Raj. 'But no snacks. It'll be time for dinner soon.' She returned to her room and resumed reading.

Raj came in, tea cup in hand.

'How was your prayer meeting?' asked Arundhati. 'Is it twice in a week? Do you ask your patients to come a little early on these days?' she asked.

Rajaraman sat on another lounge chair. 'I don't give appointments on the days of prayer meetings. Can't take a chance as some of them turn up late. Then I'll be badly stuck.'

'Even on regular days your patients have somewhat thinned out, haven't they, Raj?'

'What makes you think so? How would you know? You're out for work all day.'

'Not on Saturdays. Anyway, that's the impression of Rooprani.'

'I have my own clinic assistant to appraise the situation, thank you. Rooprani needn't go sleuthing around,' he said curtly and left the room.

He was unusually quiet at dinner. Somewhat sulky too, thought Arundhati. Perhaps she shouldn't have talked about his patients. It's none of her business. Anyway, they had both taken a decision long ago not to talk about their personal problems over the dining table, in the presence of the cook and the maid. After dinner, Rajaraman went straight to his room, without even a token 'Good night' to Arundhati. In many ways, she was glad about the arrangement. Both Rajaraman and she could get their individual space without disturbing the other person. She changed into her night clothes and waited indefinitely for Rajaraman to come. On second thought, she went over to his room.

'Good night, Raj,' she smiled, standing at the doorway.

'Ah, good night, good night, Dattie. Sleep well. Oh, I forgot to mention that I met a new Guru in the prayer meeting. Swami Govindarajulu. Won't you sit down for a moment?'

Arundhati sat on his lounge chair.

'Originally from Andhra, he is fluent in English, Hindi, even Tamil. He speaks like he is one of us! Maybe because the *ashram* he lives in is at Kanjeepuram. They've a branch here in Patel Nagar, which is where he is staying now. A very learned man. Someday, I'll call him over so you can meet, shall I?'

'By all means. He sounds like one of those amazing old timers,' smiled Arundhati. 'I've met some Telugu people who write in Tamil and are published authors. What's more, their writings are respected by their Tamil peers. But he is a Swami-ji. Will he visit private homes on invitation?' she asked.

'Actually no. He is a *sanyasi*. Still, I'll just take a chance so that you can also meet him. I think he…he may make an exceptsh…that is accept….an invite from me. He is very friendly and informal with me. We've become shor…sort of buddies,' he said, with a broad smile.

Arundhati glanced at him sharply. 'Alright, let's call him on a day I'm free.'

'Of coursssh,' he nodded, from the bed.

Back in her room, Arundhati wondered if his speech was getting slurred for some clinical reason that he is hiding from her. She had noticed it on occasions, though she didn't comment on it. Why make him self-conscious about it? She made a mental note to check with his close friends in the medical fraternity.

***

[2]

Govindarajulu came on 26 January, the Republic Day, a holiday. Arundhati noted his plump, round face and eyes that seemed to be overly eager not to miss a single detail of anything around him. Like those hawk eyes in snoopy, gossipy women. She chided herself for her ungracious thoughts about a *sanyasi*. The yellow shawl he had draped over his loose sweater had 'Sri Ram' in Devanagari printed all over it. Through those winter garments, his stomach was distended, like a potbelly. Does he have a liver problem? Oh god, why do I have such thoughts buzzing in my head, thought Arundhati, pressing her hands together in a *namaste*. 'Swami-ji, we're honoured by your visit. How kind of you to come.'

'My pleasure, entirely,' he smiled.

She had spent the entire morning personally cooking a few Tamil dishes with Rooprani helping her grind, grate, mix and assist for all those labour intensive dishes. Roop was a fast learner. In addition, she appreciated the aroma of Tamil cooking. Arundhati filled a few empty bowls with portions from the two varieties of rice, one with lemon garnished with coconut, the other with tamarind gravy garnished with roasted ground nuts called *puliyodarai*, a hot favourite with some people. She filled other utensils with *sambar*, *rasam*, *pacchadi* made with thick yoghurt and two kinds of vegetables garnished with freshly grated coconut. She stored *puris* in a covered bowl and stored some fried *appalam* in a tall, covered steel utensil. She instructed Rooprani to keep all of them on the right side of the kitchen counter.

'Don't serve anything from these items even if we fall short of food that's put out on the table, understand? They're all for you and me.'

'Why Madam-ji?' she asked, puzzled.

'Just do what I ask you to. We can't take a chance. Of course, he is a respected *sanyasi* and it's kind of him to visit our home but generally, men just gobble up everything you put out on the table without a single thought about the women, whether they have enough to eat.'

Rooprani burst out laughing. 'You're right, Madam-ji. I do this trick even in my home.'

'It's nothing to laugh about. And it's good you stash away some food for yourself and your children. Otherwise, men will eat up even their own children's share, with impunity!'

Rooprani shook her head and kept all the containers on the right side of the granite counter. Suddenly, Arundhati was gripped by a nagging doubt. All the items she had prepared were the traditional Tamil dishes. This Swami-ji is from Andhra, what if he doesn't like them?

She need not have worried. Swami-ji Govindarajulu wolfed the food down heartily, looking like he had starved for the last three days. He rolled *puris* around the vegetables and gobbled them up in no time. He swallowed large quantities of lemon rice, and then moved on to tamarind rice, chomping noisily on the roasted ground nuts. Next, he heaped a mountain of white rice on to his plate, made a kind of well in the center and poured *sambar* into it. He finished that too within five minutes. Such a sensual eater! Arundhati stood looking at him slurping the *sambar*, totally oblivious of the fact that he was being watched by both Rajaraman who was sitting across him at the table and by Arundhati. Swami-ji leaned forward on the table, took one disdainful look at the bowl of *rasam*, asked her to pour it in a cup for him and gulped it down perfunctorily, like it was more a gesture of courtesy. He reached again for *sambar* which was more solid than watery *rasam*, which is when Arundhati went to the kitchen and whispered, 'Cook one more glass of rice quickly…just in case.'

She returned to where Rajaraman sat, served him and kept a few dishes closer to his plate.

'Raju, why aren't you eating properly?' asked Swami-ji, smiling genially across the table. 'You're one hell of a lucky fellow. My daughter Arundhati is such an excellent cook,' he said, and let out a loud satisfied belch. He went on blithely to mix a mound of white rice with yoghurt and swallowed it with pickles. In the kitchen, Arundhati scooped out a portion of the *payasam* for Rooprani and herself, took the remaining portion in a big bowl and placed it in front of Swami-ji with two cups. He made short work of it. There was very little left in the bowl.

She went to the kitchen, softly closed the door and whispered to Rooprani.

'See my point now? There's no *kheer* left in the bowl. All other items have also vanished. After this, if he asks for anything more, I'll say sorry, there's nothing left.'

'But Madam-ji, how can you say that?' she asked, aghast at the idea.

'Why ever not? You just watch the fun. If it comes to that point when I'm forced to say there's nothing more left, he won't even express regret or inquire about what you or I would eat. He may just say "Oh, that's okay. I've eaten my fill" and get up with another loud belch. If that's not appalling to you, why should my keeping some food aside for us bother you so much?'

Rooprani bent her head low and muttered, 'Oh Madam-ji, this is so much like my own home. Today I've learnt a lesson from you. So often, my children and I have very little food left for ourselves.'

'Then cook a larger quantity but remember to stash away food for yourselves. Be sensible.'

Arundhati returned to the dining table, a smile in place on her face. She went to Rajaraman and asked, 'Would you like some more *payasam*?'

He said obsequiously, 'Dattie, I'm full. Please serve Swami-ji. You've done a wonderful job, like Swami-ji said. Everything is so tasty,' he gushed.

'Swami-ji, would you like some more *payasam*?' she asked.

'My dear daughter, I just had three bowls of it. Couldn't resist. It was super! Your mother has really taught you to cook very well. Each one of the dishes was excellent. The ultimate beauty for any woman is in her culinary skills. Let me wash my hands,' he said, and got up saying, '*Eeswara*, bless my daughter Arundhati, her husband Raju and this household. They're so hospitable!'

In the living room, Swami-ji helped himself to scented betel nuts and South Indian betel leaves that she had specially got from the temple. 'My daughter, may I see your shrine?'

'Certainly, Swami-ji,' said Arundhati, leading him to their small rectangular room with one large window that let in sunlight. His eyes lingered a bit on the large picture of Devi Kamakshi, decorated with a garland.

'Does Raju worship the Devi?' he asked.

'Perhaps he does,' laughed Arundhati. 'We keep different timings for puja. I'm always in a rush to leave for the university, but I make it a point to pray to Devi Kamakshi. Sometimes in the evenings, I listen to the recital of Kamakshi Suprapaadam.'

'That's very good,' said the Swami. 'You must also learn it.'

Then he gave her suggestions to change the positions of a few bronze idols within their large, carved wooden mandapam.

They returned to the living room. When Rajaraman offered to drop Swami-ji in his ashram, he recited a long *shloka* to bless them and left.

On his return, Raj chatted with Arundhati about the modifications for their shrine.

'All that is fine Raj, but let's simplify according to our needs. He is not going to come back to check.'

'Why ever not? I want to call him again. Look how happy and satisfied he was?'

Arundhati nodded and left the room.

'Plain glutton,' she muttered to herself and went to the kitchen.

'Have you eaten?' she asked Rooprani.

'Yes, Madam-ji. Everything was so tasty, I ate too much,' she smiled, very embarrassed.

***

[3]

'Raj, I'll be a bit late in the evening. I'll go to my orthopaedic straight from the university before coming home,' said Arundhati, picking up her car key with her handbag and a file.

Rajaraman nodded in her direction and buried himself in the newspaper.

Strange. For a doctor he is so indifferent to my arthritic condition, the diagnosis, the therapy and treatment, Arundhati thought, starting the car.

The day went by in a whirl of activities at the university. The project team got together for a discussion. It was invigorating to see the young ones generate fresh ideas that were in sync with the new trends in teaching. Still, she was compelled to make a list of all their suggestions to seek the approval of the Vice-Chancellor. Fortunately, the man had not totally 'dried up' even after having worked for so many years in an atmosphere that was torn apart by political factions. As a VC, he kept a sharp eye open for funds from other sources that could be ploughed into projects.

***

The visit to the orthopaedic's clinic was reassuring, even if for wrong reasons. There were so many people far younger than her in a debilitating condition. Some were caused by genetic factors, others caused by chronic conditions or neglect. To Arundhati, the doctor suggested an increase in her calcium supplements, more exercises, therapy and a diet that wouldn't worsen her condition. 'No red meat!' he said. Arundhati smiled and declared she was a vegetarian.

Raj was not around when she reached home. Arundhati gave her bags and flask to Rooprani and went to her room for a wash. Rooprani brought her tea with her favourite cheese straws and lingered on.

'The dinner menu?'

'No, Madam-ji, you've already given me the menu.'

Arundhati waited.

'Madam-ji, please don't get me wrong. That Ramu came again and I gave him a good scolding this time.'

'Why? Did he sneak in without ringing the bell?'

'Yes. And do you know why he comes in so stealthily?'

'What is it, Roop, tell me.'

'Madam-ji, he smuggles in a bottle of *sharaab* from somewhere and hides it behind the jasmine bush.'

'He what!'

'I checked after he left. I deliberately let it be there so that I would show Saab when he comes. Then Saab could have talked to the officers of the Residents Association. After I served food to Saab, I went out to bring the bottle but it was not there.'

'Oh God!'

Rooprani's eyes were moist with sympathy as she looked at her mistress. 'I...I'll ask Saab later, maybe at night, since he has gone out now,' said Arundhati. 'Did any patients come?'

'No. No one came. The clinic is locked.'

'Did you ask our maid Chameli to sweep, swab and dust before you locked it? It should also be aired. Open the windows when Chameli cleans.'

'Madam-ji, Chameli cleans it every day, but now I'll have to supervise her work because…'

'Yes?'

'She found two bottles of *sharaab* in the cupboard.'

'O God!'

'Everything will be okay, Madam-ji. Let's pray to God. Whatever happens, I'll be with you to help. As will my husband. Till the end of our lives!' she said, her voice quivering with emotion. She picked up the tea tray and left abruptly.

Now there's no need to check with any of Raj's friends about his slurred speech, thought Arundhati. Since we don't sleep in the same room, I couldn't smell that tell-tale sour smell that comes with drinking. It's obvious he has hit the bottle, like all weak men do who have lost their purpose in life. I never thought Raj, once considered an eminent doctor, would become such an aimless drifter. Doesn't want to work anymore, is not bothered about the finances for our family, is impervious to the stinging remarks of Sudhir, our only son and the way Sujata, our daughter-in-law talks about him to her parents. How come he doesn't regret forfeiting the once flourishing practice he had, after resigning as a professor and head? Where is that Dr Rajaraman, MD, MRCP? Must catch Ramu by the neck and threaten him with dismissal by the Residents Association. I must also ask Belaram, Roop's husband to keep an eye on Ramu.

***

[4]

'Dattie, if you're free in the evening after work, why don't you call the shortlisted men over? We'll select a driver. But they must come one by one, say from 6 pm onwards to 7:30', said Rajaraman.

'I don't want to bother you about that. I'll meet them on some other day.'

'Are you sure? Okay. Whoever you select, check his references and keep the salary negotiable. I'll pay the driver.'

'No, absolutely not! The driver will be on my payroll since it was my idea to hire a driver. Besides, he would mostly drive me around the university, and to other places. You're comfortable driving our other car, so you continue. Do you have patients coming in the evening?' she asked casually.

'Eh...no. I kept the evening sh...short...sort of tentatively free for these shortlisted drivers. Now that you'll be interviewing them, I might as well look up Shwa...Swami-ji. By the way, he was all praise for you. "Such a senior professor. For all her professional status, she is so humble, an epitome of feminine grace!"' said Rajaraman.

'Oh, all that gushy talk. It just shows a male gaze,' said Arundhati.

'No Dattie, he is sincere. Shall I call him over again?'

'Oh no! Please, have a heart! I was dropping dead with exhaustion that day after cooking all those traditional Tamil dishes for him. Rooprani helped of course, with the grinding, grating and so on. Raj, I just can't repeat it, nor do I want to. This arthritis is killing me.'

'All right then, I won't call him. But I'll be seeing him today. He is teaching me some new *shloka*s. Do you know he is also into astrology and face reading?'

'No.'

'He said I've a great future in religious discourse, so I should dedicate myself totally to ashram activities and forget about everything else.'

'Even your medical practice? Raj, he is just seducing you into offering free service for the *ashram*. Watch out for it!'

'You're getting cynical. Swami-ji did not lure me into the *ashram*. It was I who went in search of a mentor.'

***

'Keep the gate firmly locked after Saab goes out,' instructed Arundhati. 'Roop, there's another bell outside the gate. Allow Ramu to enter only after he rings the outer bell. Check him closely to see if he is hiding a bottle. It's best not to admit any unknown person.'

Arundhati started the car and drove mechanically, her thoughts hovering around Rajaraman. Pay the driver's salary, indeed! The next thing you know, he'll con the driver to get him drinks and this time maybe ask him to hide them behind the bougainvillea? The honks behind her car got louder. Arundhati revved up the engine and moved forward. When she reached the university, she checked her call records. One was from Dr Ramya Seshadri and another from Bimla Gupta. She'll call them back.

She sipped her mid-morning tea and called Ramya.

'Hi Ramya. Sorry I missed your call. When did you return from the US? Had a good break?'

'Arundhati, it feels so good to be back home. I'm prepping for some interviews with the clinics I had contacted. Thought I would ask you if you're coming to the *Gita* class today,' said Ramya.

'Sorry, I'm not free. Will catch up with all of you next week. Delighted to know you're back. Will talk later.'

Next, she called Bimla Gupta.

'There's another guy who would like to meet you regarding the driver's job,' said Bimla. 'This one is not very young, fiftyish, mature, with a family he really cares for.'

'That's the kind of person I want!' said Arundhati.

'Whether it's a driver, house help, gardener, whoever, I need a guy who is a true family man. He'll be more stable than others,' said Arundhati.

'Hopefully,' laughed Bimla. 'Will WhatsApp the details. Have a good day,' she signed off.

Arundhati called her Project Head for a briefing. There were four others inducted into the team. The PH promised to work in tandem with all four of them. Next, she got a call from the Pro-VC. She assured him that she would be meeting him with the relevant files and then got busy gathering her notes.

When she returned to her room, she called Rooprani.

'Doctor Saab didn't even have lunch at home,' she said. 'I've locked both the clinic and the front gate, informed Saab before he left that there are too many prowlers, so could he ring the bell please?'

'Good. Hope you had lunch and rested.'

'Yes, Madam-ji.'

'Such a nuisance, all this husband-care, after years of child-care,' muttered Arundhati.

'Madam-ji, *aap ne kuch kaha*? (Did you say something?)'

'*Nahin, nahin* (No, no). I was talking to someone who came to my room.'

She sat back, suddenly engulfed by guilt. Haven't studied even a bit for the next *Gita* class. How will she show her face to the distinguished speakers, or to Ramya, Vibha, Sandeep, others…? They'll dismiss her as a dabbler.

***

Raj, his defunct practice, his alcohol, and now his new love interest, the Swami-ji who has this huge appetite for food—all of them should be tackled firmly. She'll check the balance with their joint account in the bank, and then open an individual account in another bank, to which she will transfer some of the money from the joint account. And in future, she'll never deposit any money to their joint account. Aside from this, she did have an account in a third bank, and the house was in her name, thank god. Let me see from where he'll get the money for his drinks, or for 'donations' to the ashram. His withdrawals from their joint account is a proof of how often he has been taking money out, and not even bothering to tell me what it was for, she fumed. Rooprani said there were no footfalls for the clinic. Let me see what Raj will do when his financial resources dry up. His confidence stems from the fact that I'm working, and there is a regular income coming in.

All too often, the wives of alcoholic husbands are quickly turned into 'poor things' to 'victims' who deserve everybody's pity as they suffer in silence and shame. However, these 'poor things' continue to enable alcoholism by giving money to their tipplers. There must be a saner way of handling the problem, the stigma and the sheer helplessness that women impose on themselves in the name of a 'family'. It calls for sterner measures. Blocking off the financial resources may be one strategy.

The last time she attended the *Gita* class someone spoke about 'karmic relationship'. Under its wide spectrum, the Speaker discussed sticky, familial kinships such as parents, spouses, children and their children with a long link threading them all together. The discussions went on endlessly, spilling over the stipulated time. The speaker quipped in legal parlance that the class will 'adjourn' for now, but 'karmic relationships' can never be adjourned.

Arundhati's session with her PhD research scholar was satisfactory. The young man was diligent, earnest, and had already set his sights on applying to universities in UK and USA for pursuing his post-doctoral research. Arundhati got up and opened her handbag to take out her car key. Then she remembered that she had given the car for servicing. She called for a cab.

***

[5]

The front gate wasn't locked. Why? Has Rooprani forgotten my instructions? Arundhati opened the gate and went past the living room when she heard someone talking. She glanced through the lacy half-curtain of the front window. It was Raj sitting in the living room, talking to someone on the phone.

'I have it all worked out, Shyamal. You may say I'm lucky. I've stopped my practice so that I devote my full time to Swami-ji's teachings and his ashram work. I can afford to,' he laughed. 'My wife still has several years of service before she retires. Why don't we meet one of these days? No, no, not in my house. Let's meet somewhere else where we can...'

Arundhati stepped into the porch quietly and sat down on one of the cane chairs. She went blank. The kind of 'nothingness' that a yoga teacher or a meditation master recommends which is so difficult to achieve, seemed to have descended on her unbidden. She closed her eyes and lost count of time. Not a single sound around. Raj must've retreated to his room. Rooprani must be busy preparing dinner.

She heard the shuffling of feet.

'Madam-ji, are you alright? Shall I get you some water?' she asked.

'Ah, Roop! I'm alright. Just sat down to rest my legs. Get me tea in my room.'

'Very well, Madam-ji,' she said, picking up her handbag, flask and books.

The ginger tea was refreshing. Arundhati bit into the goodies in a bowl and poured herself another cup of hot tea. She stretched her legs on the bed in her favourite posture and closed her eyes.

'I have it all worked out, Shyamal. You may say I'm lucky. I've stopped my practice so that I devote my full time to Swamiji's teachings and his Ashram work. I can afford to,' he laughed. 'My wife still has several years of service before she retires'.

I suppose he expects me to slog on for the remaining years of my service, prioritize my work, the finances of the house, then my medical treatment. And if there is some residual time, I'll read for that occasional *Gita* class at Chinmaya Mission, make a sorry sight while the discourses go neatly over my head and occasionally—very occasionally—put out my neck like a turtle and sneak into a meeting with the Gargi Group.

'Dattie ...'

She opened her eyes and found him standing near her bed.

'Dattie...Sorry. Were you taking a nap? When did you return?'

'I wasn't taking a nap, just resting, that's all. My legs ache a lot.'

'Oh'.

Arundhati was flabbergasted. Are you a doctor at all? She thought. Have you no interest in your wife's condition, or what the orthopaedic says or what's the line of treatment?

'Raj, I can't drag on like this. It's time for me to take a hard decision. I've clocked enough years for a VRS. Even if I put in my papers now, I'll be eligible for a full pension.'

'VRS?' He looked horrified. 'Well, you surprise me, Dattie. Why VRS?'

Arundhati looked at his crestfallen face but didn't reply. Raj left the room abruptly.

'V—R—S. Voluntary Retirement for my Spiritual Pursuits' she whispered to his retreating back.

GLOSSARY

addigai: A heavy, chunky necklace that fits close around the neck like a choker, and is usually studded with diamonds and other precious stones and pearls.

Ajji: Grandmother

Akka: Elder sister.

amirtham: Ambrosia. *Amrit* in Hindi.

Ammauvare: A respectful way of addressing women as 'Amma' or mother in Kannada.

Anna: In some Kannada families, children address their father as 'Anna', while in others they call him 'Appa'. 'Anna' otherwise refers to one's elder brother in Tamil, Telugu, and other Indian languages.

Annapurni: Also called 'Annapurna' or 'Annapurneshwari', she is known as the Hindu goddess of food and nourishment and is believed to be a manifestation of Parvati.

anne: A friendly and colloquial way of addressing a man as a brother.

appalam: Deep fried snacks made of *urad dal*. *Papad* in Hindi.

bagara baingan: A spicy preparation of eggplant.

beeda: Roll of betel leaves with pieces of areca nut, clove, coconut scrapings and other aromatic ingredients.

besan: Gram flour.

biryani: A spicy dish made with rice and vegetables.

chakli: Crisp fried snacks made with rice and *urad* dal in a variety of combinations.

chapattis: Wheat bread. It's a staple food in many a household.

deodar: Conical cedar trees native to the Himalayas.

elaichi: Cardamom.

empaa: An informal way of addressing a male.

Endero Mahanu Bhavulu: A *Pancharatna Kriti* composed by Sri Thyagaraja in classical Carnatic music.

Gargi: Gargi Vachaknavi was a philosopher who is honoured as a renowned expounder of the Vedas. She was also known as Brahmavadini, a person with knowledge of Brahma Vidya. She remained celibate all her life and was venerated during her times.

gopuram: A monumental entrance tower at the entrance of Hindu Temples in South Indian architecture.

javali: Festive clothes for the wedding, especially those brought for the groom's relations.

jeera and dhania: cumin and dried coriander.

kabuli chana: A variety of chickpeas.

kalkandu: Rock-candy.

kann dhrishti: An Indian belief that one can remove 'the malevolent eye' of people by applying a black spot with kohl on the face of a healthy child.

kanna: A term of endearment, like 'darling'.

karma: In spiritual discourse, it refers to one's action. It also implies the principle of cause and effect that governs one's action and work.

karuvadaam: A salty, spicy preparation made with a combination of rice, bengal gram and other ingredients ground into a moist paste, and then dried in the sun. It is fried in oil and eaten with meals.

karuveppilai: Curry leaves.

khaad: manure

kho-kho: Traditional Indian game of tag.

koottu: Vegetables cooked with lentils and coconut.

kraambu: Cloves.

kuttu vilakku: Tall lamps traditionally designed with a carved stem that holds the lamp on top with five flowerets for the wicks.

kuzhambu: A spicy dish made with tamarind juice and vegetables.

Maitreyi: Maitreyi, 'the wise one' was an Indian philosopher who lived during the later Vedic period around 8th century in ancient India. She is one of the two wives of the sage Yajnavalkya and is mentioned in the *Brihadaranyaka Upanishad.*

Maleraaya: The god of rains, Indra.

mandapam: A decorative structure in wood or marble in which icons and pictures are kept for worship.

Manni: Wife of an elder brother; 'Bhabhi' in Hindi.

mathri: A salty fried snack made with flour.

mari: A tender term of endearment in Kannada used for small children.

marukkuzhandu: Also called southern wood, it's a leafy plant with a strong fragrance.

morkuzhambu: A spicy dish made with sour curds.

mormilagai: Chillies that are soaked in buttermilk, and then dried in the sun. They are eaten as an accompaniment to rice dishes, after frying them in oil.

Naakku setthu poivittadhu: In Tamil it implies one's 'tongue is dead' or that their palate is jaded after eating tasteless food.

namak para and mathri: Savoury snacks served with tea.

Namaskaram: To show respect by prostrating and touching the feet of an elderly person.

nanri: 'Thanks' in Tamil.

neer mor: Buttermilk.

nei: Clarified butter, *ghee* in Hindi.

ooru: Place, especially the place of birth.

pacchadi: A side dish made with yoghurt, grated carrot or cucumber or raw/ripe mangoes according to one's preference. Called *raita* in Hindi.

palapp pazham: Jackfruit.

Patti: Grandmother.

paneer and palak pakodas: Cottage cheese and spinach dipped in a batter made of chickpea flour and fried in oil.

paruppu podi: Roasted lentil that is powdered with pepper and other ingredients. It is mixed with rice and oil and is a favourite side dish in Tamil Nadu.

payasam: Traditional rice pudding made as a dessert for special occasions. *Kheer* in Hindi.

peri idatthu penn: An upper-class bride.

Periappa: Elder brother of one's father, or the husband of mother's elder sister.

Pittu: A game played with seven flat stones and a ball, usually with two teams.

poha: A popular breakfast item made with pressed rice, chopped fresh vegetables, ginger, green chilies, and garnished with lemon juice.

poriyal: Fried vegetables.

puli-nagam: 'Puli-nagam' or tiger-claw necklace is usually a pendant with two tiger claws mounted on gold that has the figure of Goddess Lakshmi flanked by two elephants. It is attached to a heavy necklace, to hold the weight of the pendant. Tiger-claws are believed to ward off malevolent spirits.

pullae: An affectionate way of addressing a small girl.

punya sthal: Sacred place.

puris: Wheat bread, deep fried in oil.

Rasam: A soup made with lentils, tomatoes and tamarind with spices.

Rasha Sundari Debi: A self-taught writer in 19th century Bengal, she lived during the times when literacy was denied to women because of a deep-rooted superstition that a woman who reads, or as much as touches a book, would be widowed. Her autobiography in Bangla titled *Amar Jiban* ('My Life') was considered as the first full-fledged autobiography written in India and was acclaimed for its lucid and readable prose.

Saab: Vernacular for 'Saheb' in Hindi; translates as 'Sir'.

Saar: Referring to 'Sir' in vernacular.

Sambar: A stew made with lentils and vegetables, flavoured with tamarind.

sandige: Crisp snacks made with rice, sago and other ingredients.

sanyasi: A renunciant, ascetic.

sappattu ramans: People who are gluttonous eaters.

satshat: Like someone has actually appeared.

saunf: Fennel seeds, eaten as mouth fresheners in the Indian subcontinent.

sharaab: Alcohol.

streedhan: Jewellery, silverware and other things given to a bride by her parents as her personal property.

sumangali: Married woman whose husband is alive. *Suhagan* in Hindi.

sumangali prarthanai: A ceremony held before the wedding to pray for the long life of the bride's husband. *Sumangali*s (married women) are invited for a feast after which they bless the bride.

t'ai chi: A Chinese martial art and system of calisthenics that has practitioners worldwide. It consists of sequences of very slow, controlled movements that are also practised for health benefits and meditation.

thalai Deepavali, thalai Pongal: The first Diwali and the first Pongal (Sankranti), after a girl's marriage. They are celebrated as special days.

thalir vetrilai: Tender betel leaves.

thangacchi: Younger sister.

Thatha: Grandfather.

Thomas Becket: The Archbishop of Canterbury who was canonised as a saint soon after his assassination in the 12th century.

til oil: Sesame oil, used in cooking.

tulsi: Holy basil.

uppuma: A salty snack made with semolina.

utthappam: A thicker variety of *dosa*, sometimes with a filling.

urad dal: Black gram.

Vanakkam: A salutation, like *namaste*, expressing respect.

vatral kuzhambu: A dish made with dried vegetables and thick tamarind solution.

VRS: Voluntary Retirement Scheme offered by the government and universities for people who have completed a certain period of work and can now opt to retire with the benefits of a full pension.

Yajnavalkya: Yajnavalkya was a Hindu sage who debated metaphysical questions such as the nature of existence, consciousness and impermanence.

Zamindar: Prosperous land owners with a huge property.

ACKNOWLEDGMENTS

Some of the stories in this collection were earlier published in different magazines and journals. I would like to acknowledge my grateful thanks for the permission granted by them for inclusion in this volume. I take this opportunity to thank *Confluence: South Asian Perspectives*, Bromley, U.K. ('Open the Gate'; 'Ladies' Watch', formerly published as 'Girl Watch'), *SETU*, Pittsburgh, USA ('Dregs'), *Indian Literature*, Sahitya Akademi, New Delhi ('Kitchen Fire'), *Muse India*, Secunderabad ('Addigai', formerly published as 'addigai'), *The Beacon*, Pune ("A' for Apple'), *Rhetorica Quarterly: A Literary Journal of Arts*, Lucknow University ('As Dapper as They Come', formerly published as 'As Dapper as They Make Them'), *Borderless Journal*, Singapore ('Floating Free'; 'Annapurna Bhavan') and *Usawa Literary Review*, Mumbai ('The Colour Green').

I thank Mrs Tultul Dey Niyogi of Niyogi Books for offering to publish this collection which is very special for me in many ways.

I would like to thank Ms Trisha De Niyogi immensely for her time and interest in designing this book so creatively along with the designers to showcase this collection of stories. Many thanks to Sri Nirmal Kanti Bhattacharjee, Director, Niyogi Books, for his interest in my manuscript and his very insightful editorial interventions and critical comments whenever I sought them. I thank Ms Anwesha Panda, my editor, for the delicate sensitivity she brought to her editing skills and for alerting me about repetitions. If my stories have clarity and lucidity, I owe them to her in a large measure.

Working with the Niyogi team has been altogether a happy experience.

Lakshmi Kannan

New Delhi